AN HONEST WOMAN

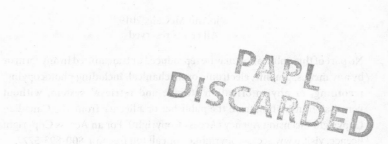

An Honest Woman

A very bookish novel

by

JoAnn McCaig

thistledown press

Thistledown Press Ltd.
410 2nd Avenue North
Saskatoon, Saskatchewan, S7K 2C3
www.thistledownpress.com

Library and Archives Canada Cataloguing in Publication
Title: An honest woman / JoAnn McCaig.
Names: McCaig, JoAnn, 1953- author.
Identifiers: Canadiana (print) 20190131373 | Canadiana (ebook)
20190131756 | ISBN 9781771871785
(softcover) | ISBN 9781771871792 (HTML) | ISBN 9781771871808
(PDF)
Classification: LCC PS8575.C34 H66 2019 | DDC C813/.54—dc23

Cover painting: *Hush* by Betsy Rosenwald
Author photo by Michelle Lazo
Cover and book design by Jackie Forrie
Printed and bound in Canada

Canadä

Canada Council   Conseil des Arts
for the Arts   du Canada

Thistledown Press gratefully acknowledges the financial assistance of the Canada Council for the Arts, the Saskatchewan Arts Board, and the Government of Canada for its publishing program.

ACKNOWLEDGEMENTS

This novel was many years in the making.

First readers Audrey Andrews and Elaine Park saw what I was trying to do and seemed to think I might be able to pull it off.

Editors and mentors who helped along the way include Helen Humphreys, Kathy Page, Merilyn Simonds, and Diane Schoemperlen.

Edna Alford totally got the mythical man of the morning.

Greg Hollingshead suggested the onion structure.

The stalwart souls of the East Village Writers Collective slogged through the marshy parts with me and helped me out of the swamp. (Thanks Sarah Butson, Karen Craig, Ron Ostrander, Tim Ryan, Elena Schacherl, and Kerry Woodcock.)

Kelsey Attard offered sensible advice and a keen eye.

Al Forrie was mesmerized by the turbulence.

Michael Kenyon was the editor of my dreams.

Jackie Forrie was a good shepherd.

Igpy Pin designed a good map.

Michelle Lazo made me look good.

Betsy Rosenwald made the cover beautiful.

Perry helped with the details.

My three sons are as necessary as sunshine and fresh air.

Both of my parents were still living when I started writing this book. I honour the memory of my father, Bud McCaig (1929 to 2005) and my mother Anne S. McCaig (1928 to 2015).

DEDICATED
to readers and writers everywhere,
with love

TABLE OF CONTENTS

A LUCID DREAM

You cannot call it love, for at your age
The heyday in the blood is tame; it's humble,
And waits upon judgment.

Hamlet 3.4.68-70

A cat approached her, a black cat. Nuzzled her arm and purred. Nuzzled insistently. And then more insistently. Nuzzled his head underneath her shirt, to her breast. She had this halter T-shirt she wore a lot that summer, just a navy jersey T-shirt but instead of a neckhole and two sleeves, there was just a kind of loop that went over her head, leaving her back bare. No bra, of course.

And this cat. Well. She doesn't know what got into this cat, she was pretty fucked up that night, and maybe she just imagined a scratchy tongue on her nipple and then the thrill and horror of a mouth filled with such sharp teeth —

For now, let's just call her JM.

Let's call this Sam's Bar and Grill, Kensington Crescent, Calgary.

So, there's this woman, JM, a writer, and one night, she met this man whose teeth didn't match. The uppers sleek, white and even, the lowers crooked and stained. He sat down next to her at Sam's Bar on a November evening and they watched, united in horror, the re-election of George W. Bush. This man, the one with mismatched teeth, enchanted JM. She'd become increasingly disaffected with her usual companions, the insouciant boozy crowd that never seemed to get her jokes. That crowd, once a viable alternative to a night at home in front of a rerun of *Law and Order*, now seemed mere wretches of the earth. Compared to him, this man she'd met. He gave her his email address while Ohio hung in the balance. Next day, not really knowing or even wondering where this sudden heat came from, just acting on it, putting herself out there in a way she hadn't risked in years, she wrote to him, "You're a lovely man, you know that?"[1]

She figured it must be long past time for some kind of upheaval when, as she left the house at 9 o'clock that Tuesday night, telling her twelve-year-old son, "I'm going out," the boy got up from the couch, set down his gaming controller, glanced at the kitchen clock and said, "At *this* hour?"

This man whose teeth don't match is English born, son of a famous man and a long-suffering woman.[2] He played rugby in boyhood, hence the teeth. He is a philosopher, currently unemployed. It shocks him, deeply, that JM has never thought to apply Hegelian dialectic to the novels of Jane Austen. This man with mismatched teeth drinks too much, smokes too much, and is almost as smart as he thinks he is. He likes to stay on at the bar after she goes home to her kids.

She wishes he'd ask her questions, though. He never seems to. In fact, now that she thinks about it, nobody asks her direct questions anymore. Sometimes, days or even weeks go by and the only thing anybody ever asks her is: *Was that to stay or to go?* The only direct question the man with mismatched teeth

---

[1] If JM were an honest woman, she'd admit that this encounter was arranged through an online dating site.

[2] Here's a story he told about his family: His mother was working as a volunteer at a silent auction. She and a co-worker watched an attractive young woman pass. The co-worker said, "Do you know the artist David Pyke? That's his girlfriend," unaware that the woman she was speaking to was David Pyke's wife.

ever asked her is: "Where are all the strip joints in this town anyway?" And sometimes, when she's out with him, he gets so drunk he embarrasses her. And, he hectors her mercilessly about the musical genius of Nick Cave and the Bad Seeds. She remains unconvinced, however.

And in the end, it seems, he remains unconvinced. About her, that is. In fact, his lack of interest in her is truly stunning. He apologizes, says he's got a lot on his mind. That's what he says but when she touches him he trembles. Not on the surface of his skin, which tenses against hers, recoils almost — but deeper, inside his body. A rumbling. A motor quietly idling.

It has been many years alone, for her. More years than she wants to count. And one night a while back, in the midst of this cruel romantic drought, she prepared a lifetime list of her lovers, chronologically, by name. The tally was respectably long, and satisfying. As she reviewed the list, it occurred to her, equally satisfyingly, that there was not one name whose pastness she regretted. There is not one man that she now misses or dreams of or longs for. She is fond of closure. It's possible she has a gift for it.

But as she thinks about it a bit more, after an evening at Sam's, she remembers two men she does regret, two men she wants more of, two she wishes she could have again. They don't have names, though. That's why they aren't on the list.

The first she met when she was nineteen, at university in Ottawa. She'd gone out with her roommates to the Chaudiere Ballroom in Hull, where they flirted with some guys and invited them home after the bar closed. The girl she shared a room with got together with one of the guys so JM had to find

12

somewhere else to sleep. The last of the men, the one nobody had claimed, sat slumped in the living room chair, snoring. She hadn't been particularly interested in any of these guys. She liked to think, then, that the power of refusal was the best card in her hand. A sign of her value, her independence. So with everybody else paired off and passed out in various bedrooms, she hauled the foamy out of the hall closet and curled up on the living room floor in a sleeping bag. Sometime during the night, though, the guy in the chair woke up and just sort of took her. All of a sudden he was just on her with such . . . authority. She had never been handled like that before, with that intensity, that strength of purpose. Reader, don't mistake this for violence or coercion. Not at all. His ardour was thrilling. The sweet intense words he breathed in her ear. His honest desire was both flattering and infectious.

He was gone when she woke up the next morning. And she surprised herself, her cynical, worldly nineteen-year-old self, by pining for that man for weeks, pining like a teenybopper. Scanning the streets for his little green sports car. An MG, she thought. Never saw him again. Doesn't recall his name, if she ever knew it in the first place.

Six months later came the other nameless man. She had dropped out of university by then and was living out on the west coast, drinking, getting high and screwing pretty much anything that moved. Because by then she had come to believe that her most potent currency was consent. A sign of her independence, her freedom. And so she gave her consent to just about any reasonably attractive guy who offered a place to sleep or a ride up the Island Highway or a square meal.

The details are foggy. She could make them up, but that would just be fiction.

There was a party at an A-frame on Quadra Island, smoke and hallucinogens and booze and, well everything seemed a little distorted, but in her memory, the cabin's main floor just had a stove and some chairs and shelves, and then the sleeping area was a loft that you climbed a rickety ladder to get to. She had climbed up to this loft under the eaves, maybe to get away from whatever was happening at the centre of the little house, the loud raw energy of the voices and guitars.

Maybe she passed out for a while, and then that weird thing happened with the cat, and after that, she must have tumbled down from the loft onto the floor of the main room, where the party was going on. And a short time later, a guy approached and pulled her away from the guitars and booze and the chest-thumping and rough laughter of the mostly men in the room. This kind man offered her a place to stay and she said okay, fully expecting him to exact the usual fee. He drove her to a little cottage near the ferry landing. The man had pale skin, and reddish blond hair. He gently put her to bed. He didn't touch her. Maybe he honestly realized that she was kind of used up, so he tucked her into a clean warm bed and let her sleep. She doesn't remember much about the next morning. Sunlight through little square-paned windows, water sparkling in the harbour. Fried eggs. A white lambskin draped over a wooden rocking chair. If she ever learned this man's name, she's forgotten it now. Never saw him again either.

It strikes JM as quite funny that it's only these two she longs for, it's only these two she wishes she could have again.

These honest men.

Death visited her, last night. Her own death. She awoke in the small hours, as she often does these days, got up, and padded down the hall to the bathroom. Produced gouts of unexpected blood, dark clots then a bright sudden swirl. Accustomed by now to random bleeds, she cleaned up quickly, and when she crawled back between the covers, the bed was still warm. She lay there listening to herself breathe. And then it stopped. Everything stopped. Breathing, heartbeat, consciousness. Life left her body. An absence, a space.

Then she breathed again.

It was just a small absence. Grey, like smoke. About half an inch long.

Tonight she dreams the familiar dream. The one about pulling up to a house in the country. A sweeping double staircase, a dog barking, someone awaiting her up on the landing, the high porch. Like always, the dream ends before she finds out what is behind the door at the top of the stairs.

This is her story, JM's story. This is the beginning of what happens when a final not flicker but conflagration of desire engulfs her, as the last hormones flare and flee. Fiery desire to love and make love and write and rise and triumph and and and —

A HAPPY PRISONER

If that I speke after my fantasye
As taketh not agrief of that I seye
For myn entente nys but for to pleye.

"The Wife of Bath's Prologue"
Geoffrey Chaucer

A NOTE TO THE READER:

In this section the narrator, Janet Mair, often tunes out of her real life and drops down into fantasy.

In the text, these forays into her dreams and fantasies are indicated by downward-pointing arrows, like these: ↓↓↓↓

When Janet returns to her real, actual (though admittedly fictional) life, you'll see sideways-pointing arrows, like these: →→→→→

I sleep late — bless this lake and its lush silence — but startle out of bed after nine, embarrassed to think that Mister Sunshine might ring the bell and I'd have to answer the door with ratty hair and pillow-seamed cheek. All quiet, though, and, right, Mister S isn't coming 'til later and the kids are still fast asleep. It's grocery day, so I make my preparations, gather the list, collect the videos. Damn kids have left a couple in the bunkhouse, apparently.

The moment I enter the room, I smell it. A sour sharp chemical smell. Sure, there are the usual crushed pop cans — the boys flex their biceps, shout at each other *hey, you got a licence for those guns?* — along with splintered potato chips, crumpled candy wrappers, but more mess, more carelessness this summer than last, when I was shocked to realize that the best week of the season was the one I'd spent with three fourteen-year-old skateboarders. Not this year. There's an edge to Matt and his friends, something nasty. And then there's the . . . something that Trev slid under a blanket when I walked in on them yesterday.

And yes, there it is.

In my day kids at least had the wit to be devious. Not this crew. A zip-lock, tucked carelessly beneath a sleeping bag. Inside, two stripped cigarette filters and a twisted sheet of paper containing dark tobacco that smells like old puke. I track the chemical smell. To the sauna. Christ almighty! A hundred acres of forest and fresh air and they have to smoke up in a

19

small enclosed space in a pristine and rigorously smoke-free bunkhouse? In the bloody sauna? The smell will cling to those cedar walls for months, years.

I'm pissed. Decide that's it, those friends of his are going back to the city today, and Matthew stays here. No, he may not drive back to town with the guys, Craig with his newly minted driver's licence. No Snoop Dogg and Buck 65 in the car, no stop at the skateboard park in Banff, no. Matthew stays here. Where he is safe.

Damn kids. Really cramp a person's style. Like the way two weeks ago I forgot all about Leland's kids when I was writing that really hot scene between him and my central character Jay in the Kensington Suites. There they were, Leland and Jay fucking like animals over every square inch of that suite and afterwards he's going to spirit her away to some lovely little cottage in Suffolk or Sussex or somewhere to get away from the press, and Jay will heal him and love him and help him be strong. But then I remembered, what about his kids? He can't just take off and leave them to deal with the death of their mother on their own. I mean, the Leland I'm creating is a bit of a bastard, but not that bad.

Damn kids. Ruin everything.

All told, the chores take all morning. Hope I haven't missed Mister Sunshine; he's the guy my ex-father-in-law, Dad Moe, hired to install a solar heating system for the water tanks in the cabin. Mister S, a twenty-first century diviner, is a startlingly handsome man in his thirties — trim and tanned and glowing with sincere environmental goodness and grand health. He wears khaki hiking shorts and a white T-shirt emblazoned with the company logo, which of course incorporates a smiling sun. Me, I never manage to get much further than quietly fretting about the environment, but I admire (also fear) those who roll up their sleeves and get to work on the problem. And, as with any good-looking man I meet, I begin by assuming indifference if not outright rejection and just carry on from there. It's a stance that usually serves me well.

I first met Mister Sunshine two weeks ago, when my friends were here. Our month at the cottage this year goes like this: my youngest, Eric, with his little buddies the first week, then my friends the second; Darce and her boyfriend for part of the third week (all they could spare from summer jobs before heading back to university), and now Matt and his gang, Eric tagging along, good as gold, to close off the month. Dad Moe has never wavered on the cabin, ever. "You are still my daughter-in-law; these are my grandchildren. You are entitled to your time at this place."

I remember waking up that first Mister Sunshine morning two weeks ago with lines from Hamlet in my head, punk kid pontificating to his mother about her unseemly lust, some nonsense about the heyday in the blood being tame. Then, while Paula and Manjini and I lounged on the deck, talking of ceramic museums in Meissen and Guangzhou, exploring the relationship between John Cage and mixed-ability dance, debating whether maintenance enforcement is worth the trouble when saddled with a deadbeat ex-husband, suddenly this lovely man appeared on the deck. Oh how he smiled, particularly at me, I thought. I couldn't figure out why, but I liked watching him anyway. That day he worked in the bunkhouse, because, he explained, the installation required a short-term interruption of the water supply, and he didn't want to inconvenience anyone. My mood was bright. So I smiled back at Mister Sunshine, said, "Feel free to take a swim break whenever you like. It's gonna be a hot one."

Later on, in that restless lull in the middle of a summer's day, I sat on the deck while my friends napped. Watched Mister Sunshine stretched out on the raft and wondered if he had a towel. Wondered if I should offer him one. It didn't occur to me then — that would come later — to imagine towelling him off myself. With my own hands. With my tongue. No, that came later. Soon enough, but a bit later. I was still in the sweet stuff then, with my characters Leland and Jay. Things were still under control.

So, in the manuscript I'm working on, working title *Final Draft*, I knew somebody had to die to bring Jay over to the UK, to deepen it and make them take the risk. At first I had Leland's wife bump herself off — like Rochester's in *Jane Eyre*, how convenient — but then I thought, why not make it Leland's daughter? Sure, this is a loss Jay would truly sympathize with, because of her own sister . . . So even though they stay in the suite — they have to because of his other kids — it is still sweet and good but then. But then something happens.

Wow, Jay's and Leland's story is getting weirder, more intense. I revised the up-against-the-door scene, the "there you go" scene — oh how I've gone over and over that one in my mind with great pleasure ever since it occurred to me in the car on the way home from the last department meeting of term, rush hour. And now the Kensington Suites scene . . . But I can't let things end in London like this, can I?

When I return to the cabin from shopping in town, the yellow van with the sunny smiling logo is nowhere in sight. The boys are finally up, though, draped over the furniture like throws. I ask them to help bring the groceries in. They don't move. I ask again. Still no response — gang mentality, first guy to blink. Only when I walk over and switch off the TV in the middle of their Simpsons video do they get to their feet and slouch towards the door, though by this time, poor little Eric has made three trips — way more than his share. I remind myself to spend some time with him today. Between the manuscript and these damn teenagers, I've neglected the poor little guy. But Matthew must be dealt with first. I decide to hold off until after lunch, and I've already popped a cookie sheet full of bacon into the oven when Dad Moe finally returns my call.

I've been worried about him, but he says he's fine, he has forgotten his favourite pen at the cabin, though, and wants me to bring it back to town with us when we return.

I get off the phone just in time to discover that the bacon is burnt. But at least the eggs and hash browns are okay, and I set the boys to work making toast and cutting watermelon. I'm chipping blackened bits of pork fat off the surface of the pan, wondering how a multimillionaire could fret about a lost pen, when it occurs to me that it is precisely because of his attention to such details that he's as rich as he is.

The doorbell interrupts our sullen greasy meal and there he is, beaming. Mister Sunshine. He stands braced against the doorjamb, which shows his muscular arms to advantage, and I can't help thinking, *Got a licence for those guns?* Mister S, clean and shining and smiling warmly, in his trademark khaki and white. He has thick curly reddish-brown hair, a thick curly beard. Burnished is the word that comes to mind. I stand at the door, certain that I have a flax seed stuck prominently in my bridgework.

"Feeding teenagers," he says, peering over my shoulder. "I was just out on the coast visiting my kids. Man, I couldn't believe how much these kids eat, eh?"

I concur, "Keeping food in the fridge is practically a full-time job. Had to make another grocery run this morning. I hope you didn't arrive earlier?"

"Oh no, just finished up another job down the road."

"Well. The basement door's open, so please just go ahead. I'll be around if there's anything you need. A bit chillier today, so you probably won't even want a swim."

"Probably not," he says, "but you never know. Weather can change pretty fast around here."

"It sure can," I say. I'm wondering why he's still standing there. Once he goes away, perhaps I can try to figure out what he means. Perhaps there are those who can figure out what people — particularly men — mean while actually in conversation with them. But I am not one of those.

Kids. Visiting kids on the coast. So they don't live with him.

He says he'll have to turn the water off for a while; in fact he has explained this several times. I say, "Oh no, really, just go ahead. Give us a little notice and we'll fill the sinks and a couple of buckets for the toilets."

He is being excessively solicitous about avoiding inconvenience, I think. Could it possibly be that he just wants to keep me talking?

No. That couldn't be it.

Mister S grabs his toolbox and heads down to the basement. The boys shovel food into their mouths, without pleasure, conversation, or thanks. I ask Trev and Craig to do the dishes and say to Matt, "I need to talk to you. Let's go for a walk."

I wouldn't have noticed the yawning, if my sister hadn't mentioned it after Matt's visit out east last summer. "A nervous tic, you've probably never noticed it," she said. "He yawns when he's anxious in social situations, or stressed."

"He does?"

"Yeah, it's bizarre. A friend of mine commented on it, and then I started to notice it too. If he's feeling awkward, he just yawns and yawns. Obviously, he's never anxious around you, but — "

So there we are, Matt and me, walking up the road from the cabin, the dog prancing happily before us, toward the gate. And Matt yawns constantly for the entire twenty minutes we're together.

I start out, "When I went into the bunkhouse this morning, I — oh hello, how are you today?"

A neighbour. An intense crazy neighbour, senior citizen, whose face lights up at the prospect of someone to greet, and Matt and I stand politely, hearing tales of his brilliant son and talented grandchildren, all the while trying to inch around, circle dance him back towards his cabin and get ourselves pointed back up the road. It takes a few minutes, but we manage it. The trick with the elderly is to let them talk as long as they keep bragging, but to make a fast break when they start complaining about the government or young people on drugs.

25

We walk on and I count ten steps, but he can't take the suspense. "So, what's up?"

"Matt, I found drug paraphernalia in the bunkhouse this morning."

He yawns and yawns. "This is awkward," he says.

"I'm worried because it was a smell I didn't recognize. I mean, look, I know it's normal for kids your age to . . . mess around with cannabis, but — "

"Did *you*? When you were in high school?"

"Well, yeah. But if it's something else, then that's a real concern for me. The smell was really — "

"It's Colts, these cigarillo things. Trev brought them. Craig didn't even do it, it was just me and Trev."

"Matt, now I know for sure that you're lying. Because the first night you guys got here, and you went out for a canoe ride, I heard Craig say, 'Wow, everything's so much cooler when you're high.'"

"How did you hear that?"

"I was out on the deck. You know how sound carries on the lake. I heard every word you guys said."

Yawn. Yawn. Yawn. "This is really awkward."

"Sure is. And I was so mad this morning! I was going to just send the guys home — "

"But Mom — "

"Matt, how could you do that? You have asthma. You must never smoke anything, ever. And why in God's name would you smoke that stuff in a little closed room in a house where you know nobody ever smokes, ever? What were you thinking?"

"I don't know, Mom. I'm sorry. It won't happen again."

26

"Well, you guys have lost the use of the bunkhouse for the duration. You need to be in the house, where I can keep an eye on you."

"I know, I know. Okay."

"So. I guess we're good, then. And you guys are going to behave?" I'm such a goddamn coward, can't face the thought of Matt sulking around the house staring daggers at me for three days.

"Yes. Boy, this is awkward. It was just . . . a little weed, that's all. The smell was from the Colts."

The sun has come out, and when Matt and I return to the cabin, the other two boys have taken Eric out to the raft. Matt changes into his swim shorts and paddles out to join them. I wander down to the beach, begin picking weeds and gathering water toys. Their voices carry clearly, despite the breeze, and I hear the questions even before Matt pulls himself onto the raft.

"What did she say?"

"She knows."

"Everything?"

"Pretty much."

"Oh man."

"What did she say, though?"

"I, uh. I can't say much more. Because of — " Eric, of course. Bless him, I think. Matt's a good kid still.

They lower their voices, now. But after a few moments, Trev dives off the raft and swims purposefully to shore. Emerges from the water and stands on the dock. He has something to say. "Um," he begins. I always tell the friends of my children to call me either Mrs. Mair or Janet, but most of them simply choose to call me nothing at all. Or "Hey" or "Um." Trev continues, "Hey, I'm sorry about what happened. It was my fault. Matt's not like that."

I am eager to believe this statement, without examination, and despite knowing that Trev is a smooth liar. I realize how smooth when I remember coming in to the bunkhouse last night to call the boys to dinner — and watching them emerge from the sauna, Matt and Craig red-faced and clumsy, but Trev sliding out last, his bedroom eyes heavy-lidded, saying, "You're right, guys, we need to heat up those stones a little longer. It's nowhere near hot enough." I'd caught them in the act then and there, without knowing it.

And okay, perhaps the fact of a bare-chested young man dripping lake water —

Yes, yes, it comes on, this arousal, this awakening . . . all I know is I just really want this conversation to end, so I say, through an armload of weeds, "Well. That's good to hear. But we've got some pretty basic ground rules around here, and you guys broke a whole bunch of them."

"I know. I'm sorry. It won't happen again."

"Well. Make sure it doesn't, and I won't tell your parents."

"Oh, they know already."

"They do?"

"Yup. Um, would you mind if I go back in the bunkhouse for a minute? I just need to grab a shirt I left in there."

"Go ahead, Trev. But make it fast, okay?"

I toss the weeds onto the pile and begin to gather up the broken bits of Styrofoam noodles that litter the beach; the boys used them yesterday as lightsabers in a Star Wars battle.

28

Oh how they hang suspended between boy and man. And I am here, a witness. I remember to feel thankful for that.

Just to get away from Trev, I trudge up the embankment and into the basement. I'd forgotten about Mister Sunshine, but there he is, crouched over his pipes and panels, wrench in hand. His smile is warm, like sunshine. His name, of course, is Ray.

"Damn kids," I mutter, dumping the broken noodles in a corner.

"I know what you mean," he replies. "My son's twenty and still living with his mom, not doing much of anything. But my daughter's fifteen going on thirty, she's so sensible."

I am trying to do several things at once — trying not to worry about drug overdoses and fire damage, trying not to be a dirty old lady, and trying to do some quick math. Twenty? Even if he'd fathered this child at eighteen, that means he's gotta be at least —

And the words, the tone of "his mom" comes through loud and clear. A man who is still living with the mother of his child does not say "his mom" like that. Mister Sunshine turns to his work and I observe the backs of his tanned legs. He can't be a runner. Runners' legs look like somebody stuffed a squared-off two by four in the flesh behind the shinbone, but his are rounded, one could even say voluptuous. Then he sets down his wrench and turns back to speak to me again. Something about his daughter, bored at school, how he wants her to come out here to live with him.

This man seems to want to engage me in conversation, tell me things about himself, introduce himself. This confuses me, and I end up obeying the strongest of my several impulses: I decide that I have something else terribly important to do, if only I could figure out what that is. Oh yes —

"Well. Guess I'd better make sure that those maniacs haven't drowned my youngest yet — "

But there Eric is, down at the beach at the end of the bay. He has left the big boys muttering together on the raft and paddled over to the shore on his boogie board. I walk along the water's edge to him, call, "What's up, bud?"

"Just making a new staff," he says, testing the stick in his hands.

"That looks like a good one," I say. "It's nice and smooth because the beavers have stripped all the bark off. Look, you can see the marks from their teeth."

"Cool. Stand back, Mom." And Eric sets his face and solemnly swings the stick through the air with all the warrior grace he can conjure. He supplies the sound effects expertly: *unh, ah, hmph.*

"Looks great," I say.

"Yeah," he says. "It's always good to imagine it out before you do it."

"Yes, honey. I like to do that too."

And I'm standing there looking at my son, and the backdrop of forest behind him, and wham, I'm imagining it out myself:

News item: *Quill and Quire*

A new Canadian novel has created an international stir, by presenting a romance between a supposedly fictional British novelist (male) and an up-and-coming Canadian woman writer. Though the main character is called Leland Mackenzie, most readers quickly recognize a certain renowned author and recent recipient of the Booker Prize. The novel, published under a pseudonym, has been attributed to many established Canadian women, but none have come forward to claim authorship thus far. However —

Eric's voice snaps me back to the beach. "So can we, Mom? Can we go to the cliffs?" Ah yes, though the sun has gone under, the big boys are now clamouring for a cliff-jumping excursion, and I agree, as long as they let me drive the boat. I'd much rather sit on the deck up at the cabin with my book, but I can't trust them, today, not to do something stupid.

As indeed they do, or rather continue to do. They decide, for reasons which remain obscure, to jump off the cliffs together, like Charlie's Angels, dressed not in their usual half-mast cutoffs and boxers, but in these retro jumpsuits that someone left in the back bedroom closet decades ago — this ludicrously faux athletic wear in zippy colours, the embodiment of every-thing foolish and trivial of the late 70s: bands and stripes of colour, bright yellows, hot pinks, swooshes, drawstrings. When Darce arrived last week with her boyfriend Leo, the first activity my daughter suggested — before a swim or a wakeboard or even just a drink on the deck — was, "Hey, let's try on those old clothes!" My childhood dressups were all about the serious business of being beautiful, of rehearsing womanhood. With these kids, it's all a big friggin' joke — their costume wearing has a nastiness, a hard irony.

Darce is a handful at the best of times — the mother/ daughter thing of course — but her prickly nature pumps up the volume on that as it does on just about everything. We get along better now that she's away at university most of the year, but I often think that the two who remain to me are the beneficiaries of all the mistakes I made with Darce — the manipulations, the guilt. I've learned to disengage a little better, now. But not without the expense of sleepless nights and raging days and a current relationship with my firstborn that dances into what modern psychology would probably call projection, or maybe enmeshment.

And oh how my dreamy dreams got derailed, last week, by the factual presence of young lust. Of course, I'd warned Darce and Leo in advance that they were not permitted to sleep together at the cottage. Thus Leo was pointedly assigned the top bunk in a room shared with the boys, while Darce herself was to sleep in the back bedroom at the end of the corridor. The young couple scrupulously observed this injunction — by making out hungrily in every room of the house except the one where their ardour would not be on display, namely Darce's. They'd loll about on Leo's bunk as well — the younger boys lingering embarrassed at the door in dripping wet swimsuits, too shy to interrupt. Perhaps Darce and Leo saw themselves as refusing to be sneaky, but it looked like exhibitionism from where I stood, and it pissed me off on several levels, not least because it made my own preoccupations look empty, foolish, shameful. I was so glad when Darce and Leo finally left, and I could return to my dreamy dreams.

So, let's say, soon after the publication of *Final Draft*, a letter arrives in the mail. From him, the man who inspired my central character Leland. He writes, "I stumbled across a short story collection you published a few years back, while I was visiting Canada this summer. I must say I enjoyed it very much indeed."

My cautious reply takes about twenty-five drafts over two nights. His easy response takes a month. But it says, "I have accepted a last minute invitation from the Toronto festival, replacing a far trendier Brit who apparently got a better offer. Now, I realize that the exotic place you live, in the rain shadow of the Rocky Mountains, is not exactly a suburb of Toronto, but it would be lovely to meet you if you happen to be in attendance at the festival."

A month after that, I meet him face to face in a bar near the festival venue. He's charming and pleasant, disarming me with a gossipy yet wide ranging and intelligent overview of the season's Canadian books. Then he says:

"Actually, one of the strangest books to come out of your country in a long time is a novel called *Final Draft*. Have you heard of it?"

"Yes. I believe I have."

"Well, it's odd. A highly eroticized romance between two writers, one a Canadian woman, the other an Englishman, slightly older. The puzzling thing is, quite a few people seem to think that the English chap, the love interest if you will, is me, poorly disguised. Have you heard about this?"

I struggle not to react to the word *poorly*. "No. I hadn't heard that. How strange."

The man sits back, sips his whiskey, regards me over the rim of his glass. "Truth be told I rather envy the son of a bitch, this 'Leland Mackenzie'. He gets a lot more action than I ever do."

"I expect that you do pretty well," I murmur.

"True enough," he says. "But the most persistent question, though, is the identity of the author of the book. Have you followed the story at all?"

"A little." *Don't blush don't blush don't —*

"And?"

"And what?"

"Excuse me, Ms. Mair, but you appear to be blushing."

"Hot flash."

"I see. In any case, a lot of people have suggested, lately, that this, what's the female character's name, Jay McNair? — and yes, I got all the *Jane Eyre* references, by the way, Janet. You teach English, don't you? At a little college out west? I should say that I found the Bronte stuff rather witty — "

"Thank you" is on the tip of my tongue, but I choke it back.

"You started to say thank you, just now."

I clear my throat, shake my head, searching for something, anything, some strategy — "Actually, my little college has a student population of about fourteen thousand."

"Really? How interesting. But where was I? Oh yes, the notion that this Jay McNair is a thinly disguised version of yourself." His arched eyebrow is truly adorable.

To distract myself, I press on, "I'm curious how it affected you to see yourself as a created character?"

"It is a kick. Uncomfortable with the press. Occasionally maddening."

34

"Why maddening?"

"You, I mean she, she gets it so bloody wrong. Energetic writing though." He's watching my face, watching me very very closely indeed. I say nothing, fold my arms. Try to stare him down. He likewise folds his arms, mirroring, then plays his best card: "Right, then. The name of the supposed author of *Final Draft* is your grandmother's maiden name."

"Shit. I mean, what a coincidence."

He says, "I'd say it was pretty wet of you, if I hadn't done the same thing myself."

"You published under a pseudonym?"

"Yes. Early days. Two thrillers. It paid the bills for a few years."

"Under what name?" I ask.

"No comment," he replies.

I sip my drink. "So. My dirty little secret. A desire to be known that has to be buried but can't be denied. How did you find the genealogy on me, anyway?"

"Oh, a website called — oh no you don't — " he says.

Outside, walking back to the hotel, the two of us laughing and talking together. He says, "Too bad you're not Jay McNair. I bet she'd take me back to my room and show me a good time."

"Well, you can take her home anytime you like. She travels light." I touch his arm. "Besides, she's probably way better in the sack than I could ever be. Such things tend to be enviably ecstatic and easy for fictional characters. None of the grunting and sweat and stained sheets of real life. The me who writes is a way better person than the everyday me."

"Ah yes, the godlike writer, creating impossible bliss — "

"No, not like your little snip, what's her name, the meek little author in that blockbuster of yours — "

"You really hated that novel of mine, didn't you?"

"There are some I like better, put it that way. But what I said was 'the me who writes,' who is engaged in the process. That's quite different from The Writer, The Author — the public figure. Who is often a real asshole. Ego big as a house. All persona. I heard Carol Shields read once, and in the Q&A, someone asked her whether she enjoyed these book tours, and she said, 'Towards the end of a tour, sometimes, I hear my own voice, reading and answering questions, and I just think, *Oh god, there's that woman again.*'"

He nods. "Philip Larkin called it 'going about pretending to be myself.' He never did readings, ever." He pauses on the sidewalk, stretches, grins. "So. Janet. How many dates does it take, generally speaking, to get the average Canadian girl, the 'me who writes,' in between the sheets?"

It's in the boat, though, watching Matt and his friends clamber up the rock face in their silly ensembles that it occurs to me: hey, wait. Mister Sunshine. He's *real*.

The boys line up along the top of the cliff — their harsh laughter, the pumping testosterone. The sun's gone under and the wind feels cold, not just autumnal but wintry. They line up on the cliff edge —

If this is a real guy, I think, and he really is trying to —

Loud laughter. I have been instructed to capture the moment on Trev's video camera. I can't seem to get it focused, though, and my hands tremble with cold.

If I'm reading Mister Sunshine right, then —

I bring the boys into focus. The cliffs rise thirty feet above the lake. The water below is deep green. But something happens. Suddenly, with a rough yell, one of the boys is falling. My son teeters and swears, Trev grabs his arm and pulls him back, but Craig stumbles then falls over the cliff edge, a tumble of hot pink. Somehow, as he falls, he manages to use a hand then a sneakered foot against the rock, finding momentary purchase enough to push himself away from the cliff-face. He lands awkwardly but safely in deep water, comes up spluttering and yelling curses. Mild ones though. "You bastard, Trev, goddammit. I could kill you, you — " Even in this extremity, he's mindful of Eric and me, avoiding the F word, a kind of miracle in itself, really. Maybe he's not such a bad kid after all. Maybe none of them are such bad kids.

Naturally, once the adrenalin settles, they all want to know if I caught it on tape. No, I didn't. So, despite the cold and the scare, they want to perform a few more feats: a back flip, a twist. Then they can't wait to get back to the cabin, to sit in front of the TV to watch the recording I've made of their exploits. That's what these kids do. They go outside, do something, tape it, then race back inside to watch the movie. I think of that song from Steely Dan, back in the 70s. Was it called "Showbiz Kids"? Yes, something about the heedlessness and selfishness of the young. I never could figure out what the next line meant. I always heard it as either "love's wages" or maybe "Las Vegas," neither of which makes much sense.

But Mister Sunshine. He told me about himself, about his kids. Who live with their mother, elsewhere. There could be many reasons why he has told me these things. Perhaps he's lazy and just looking for an excuse to stop working for a while. Perhaps he's sensed or even witnessed part of my day from hell with these teenagers and wants to give me a break. Perhaps he overheard me in the shower, earlier today, saying hello to myself, as I do a lot these days. But if it's what might be called "interest" then why the hell am I running? And if this is what my fevered dreams tell me I want, then why in god's name don't I —

But Mister S is gone when we return from the cliffs. He's finished his work for the day. On the picnic table is a note, saying he'll call to arrange a time for the final phase of the job.

News Item: *The Calgary Herald*: Q&A with local author Janet Mair

CH: Ms. Mair, are you familiar with the runaway bestseller *Final Draft*?

JM: I've heard about it, but I don't read romances. Ever.

CH: Would you care to comment on the suggestion that you, in fact, are the author of *Final Draft*?

JM: Me? You must be joking. If you were at all familiar with my work, you'd realize that I could never write something like that. I've heard there's a rape scene in which the woman suddenly decides to 'lie back and enjoy it,' as some of our more benighted judges sometimes advise victims of sexual assault. You know, I think this book was probably written by a man. No self-respecting feminist would ever produce that kind of crap.

It's the last night for Matt and his friends — they all have summer jobs to return to. I make a farewell dinner of barbecued chicken and garden veggies. And for a change, the boys attempt conversation at the meal. My polite questions about school, about plans for the future, are met with elaborate shrugs, however, and they offer instead amusing anecdotes about urban-legendary gang fights, reckless behaviour, and feats of underachievement. Lord, I think, how tiresome the young are.

My young surprise me, though, by actually offering to do the dishes tonight, so I beckon the dog for another walk, scooping up the garbage bag on my way out, and carrying it out to the bear-proof bin at the side of the house. Beside, not inside, the garbage can, I notice an object. It appears to be the water bottle I'd seen this morning in the sauna. Looking more closely, I see that it is not a water bottle at all but an improvised pipe. The hole cut in the side, the rolled-up paper spout, stinking of strong tobacco and cannabis. Of course. This is the "shirt" Trev wanted to retrieve. How terribly well he has concealed the evidence. When Trev assures me that his parents know that he does drugs, I suspect that for once, he has actually told me the truth.

I walk the dog and then park myself in my favourite deck chair, with a mug of tea in my hand, to watch the dusk fall. The wind has dropped, as it usually does in the evenings here, subsiding to a breeze that shifts direction minute to minute. The air is soft and warm now. Though I'm aware of the boys huddled around the VCR inside the cabin, it's peaceful out here on the deck. I can hear the mother loon calling her young one to safety — summer's end, or nearly. A breeze rustles through the long needles of the ponderosa pine. Swallows stutter-fly above the smooth water. I have decided to forget Mister Sunshine — a silly idea in the first place. I'm sure I'm just imagining things.

↓↓↓↓↓

So we're walking back to the hotel, the Englishman and me, laughing and talking together like old friends. He says, "Tell you what. Why don't we give them something to talk about? You know that you're not the author of *Final Draft*, and I certainly believe your sincere denials of that scurrilous accusation. But what about this? What if you and I were to feed the rumour mill? Parade around the festival together? Indulging in a few well-placed gestures? Holding hands, like this, say? And imagine the press if I did something like this?"

"Aah." My knees tremble, I'm going to fall down.

"It could cause quite a sensation, don't you think?"

"Just a sec." Can't breathe. "I have a question."

He chuckles, adorably.

I'm swimming against an irresistible current, but I fight my way back. "Why should we? The only person who'll benefit is the anonymous sappy romantic with an excessively rich fantasy life who actually wrote the damn thing. I'm convinced it's a guy, aren't you? They're the real saps for romance. And that bondage scene? That could only have been written by a guy."

He grins. "You told me you hadn't read it. But never mind. We'll do it because any press is good press. My latest has sold slowly, despite respectful reviews and an excerpt in The

New Yorker. And your book of short stories deserves more attention, I think — "

Dusk deepens, darkens, and the swallows give way to the flutter of bats, hunting mosquitoes, bless 'em. The silence deepens too, and I have the strangest feeling of, I don't know, emptiness? Maybe just relaxation. Surprising after this bumpy ride of a day.

I shift in my chair, swing my feet up onto the bench, let my legs relax, knees out. And something begins to happen. I let go, feel the muscles stretch and become . . . receptive, somehow. And perfectly still. I notice how tightly my hand clutches the mug, and will it to loosen. It does. My head drops back. I listen, listen. The lap of water on the shoreline. Birds call, the horses amble down to the bay for an evening drink. Soon, the owls.

The sensation begins in my thighs — an opening, a tingling — cells dance, lively and awake, yet oddly still too. I throw my head back farther, let my knees drop, let it come. Night air moves on my skin, the light touch like a tongue. Sensation washes over me, nipples harden, mouth softens and opens. This lovely place offers itself to me unreservedly and I receive it — body and soul, gasping with pleasure.

I'm going crazy, right off the deep end — that must be it. All this love, this terrible wonderful love: an image swims up, a tall dark-haired thin Englishman, standing on the porch of the farmhouse he rents in France every summer, cup of morning tea in his fine white hands, something strange crossing his mind — a dark place in the mountains, sky black, strange whispering sounds, and some small shy creature, a woman —

The first golden sliver of full moon glows over the top of the mountain. Above it, a puff of black cloud.

I call to the boys, "Moon's coming up. Check it out!" And they make their way, grudgingly, out on to the deck. We stand and watch the rising of the moon, but the older boys can give the glimmering sky only a few minutes of their attention. Eric really gets it, though: "Wow, that cloud looks just like an eagle standing on the mountain — "

"Yes," I say, "and the moon like a spotlight behind it!"

"Cool!"

But the day has been too chilly to tempt anyone into a moonlight swim, so the boys head back indoors, and —

— and after a while my body and soul open once again to the wind, I become prayerful and again I picture him, or am I just writing, I don't know anymore — dreaming, living, fantasizing, writing, it all bleeds together — what is wish, what is prayer, what is just writing, just making things up. But I think his soul hears mine. A shriek in the trees, a bat. The wind. The caress of the wind and the rise of the moon with a cloud in front of it shaped like an eagle taking flight and my prayer my prayer my prayer —

When the boys call out to me to come inside and play a board game, I'm pulled up from a soft and drowsy place, unwillingly. But I'm dutiful. If they're going to make an effort, I must match it. *Balderdash.* Best liar wins. The game begins cheerfully, but all too soon descends into crudity and raucousness, and I shut it down. Eric toddles off to his bunk, the older boys reassemble before the TV and I drift off to my room. Lie in bed, listening to Eric cough in his bunk down the hall. Poor little guy, sits around ignored, dreaming his glorious battles. And coughing. Forest fires weren't bad this year; maybe it's the dampness. Rain, wind, more rain. This whole week, one storm passed and the next just rolled over the mountain, right behind. I'm drowsy, but can't fall asleep, not for a long time.

Two mornings later, Eric and I pack up. Those stupid boys left early yesterday without a word of thanks, without a goodbye. How deeply scary it was to think of them in a vehicle, Craig's mom's Toyota, on a highway, on their way to do dangerous things, helmetless, on large slabs of concrete at the skateboard park in Banff. In a car driven by Craig, a newly minted driver who turned 16 just last month. They didn't strip their beds or pick up their towels, either, so Eric and I work away, me egging him on with the promise of pancakes at the truck stop near the Flats on our way home.

Is the end of every summer like this, I wonder, or have I just forgotten? The initial euphoria of demand-free days giving way to a cranky ennui, impatience with the slightest domestic chore. That first sensual rush of spending whole days near naked, skin and hair exposed to air and sun and wind, sleeping under a thin sheet, windows open to the night breeze; now this same skin coarsened with sunburn, pocked with insect bites and heat rash, heels calloused from going barefoot. Tired, pissed at bad weather, pissed at my kids and hating the merest thought of going back to the city. Jesus. And all day yesterday the lower back tug of an impending bleed, but I pay no attention to these signs anymore, they mean absolutely nothing, they're a con. Sensations and moods that used to reliably predict what my body would do no longer signify. The signs mislead.

And this first draft of my novel tugs at me. I've tried but I can't leave them, Jay and Leland, there at Kensington Suites. There are scenes I can't bear to part with. My Jay. Yes, like Jane Eyre she's little, poor and plain, like Jane she's hungry. At the literary dinner party, there'll be no talk of governesses, though, and Jay won't slink off, "a little depressed." Oh no.

And then Leland comes west like some Columbus or something.

And then she goes over there for her Orange Prize — well, why not?

Hey, but how did she end up in London for a reading that first time? The up-against-the-door "there you go" time? That would never happen. Nobody in England would give a rat's ass about a sensitive little prairie novel like *Richdale*. Not unless Leland made a few calls —

The phone snaps me out of it. "Hi, it's Ray. From Mister Sunshine."

"Oh." Clear throat. "Well, how are you today?"

"Great thanks, just wanted to check in about coming over to run those tests."

"Right, yes. Well, today would probably be good. We're just packing up to head back to the city now, should be gone in an hour. So the house will be empty."

"Oh. Well. Too bad." Am I imagining *that*? That's regret, that's disappointment or I don't know, *something* —

"Yes," I say, "end of a summer. It's a sad day all right. I'm just heading out for one last swim."

"Last swim of the season," he sighs.

"Well, yes. But, there's always next summer."

"Is there?" asks Mister Sunshine. "As you get older, you begin to realize how the number of summers you might have left is dwindling down."

"I know what you mean."

"My parents just live up the road a ways from your place," he says. "I've been working around this area for about ten years now. I've been around for a while, I mean."

"That's good. You're lucky."

"So."

"So." What now? What am I supposed to say? "So. Hope it all goes well."

"I'm sure it will." He appears to be trying to make conversation. To convey *something*, but all that really comes through perfectly clearly for me is my own panic, so I take a deep breath.

"Okay then. Let's see. You know where the key is, right? Hope it goes well today, Ray. Take it easy. Bye."

I set the phone on the cradle, stride down the hall and into the bathroom. Shut the door, sit on the can, head in hands. Moaning, shaking my head: dear god, dear god, this a real guy goddammit, what the fuck, oh man —

Or maybe I get an email, supposedly from this agent in the U.K. Says he's interested in purchasing rights to my book.

Because screw pseudonyms, I'm brave enough to publish *Final Draft* under my own name.

Anyway, this literary agent, he's going to be in town next week, wants me to meet him at the Westin, in the lobby lounge, Thursday at three. Coincidentally my one day off from teaching. I dress in a floral skirt, white sweater, black stockings and flats. A trench. It's October.

I enter the near-empty bar and sit on a banquette, facing outwards, to watch for a man who described himself as "a dapper little English gent, you'll spot me." I have ordered, received my drink and am trying to look calm and self-assured when the only other customer in the place, a tall, dark-haired man slouched over his newspaper at the bar suddenly straightens, slides himself off the stool and approaches my table.

"Waiting for someone?" Voice more trebly than the one I've heard reading, being interviewed on the radio. And eyes much kinder than any I've ever dreamed. I sit speechless as he, yes, the Englishman, pulls up a chair and sits regarding me with friendly curiosity, like a toddler encountering an upended Junebug.

"You," I splutter. "Oh god. You set me up, didn't you? The whole agent thing was — "

A nod. He reaches into his jacket and I flinch. He notices, and laughs. He leans forward, smiles slyly. "Don't be afraid. I promise I won't hurt you. I was hoping you'd inscribe this for me," and tosses his copy of *Final Draft* on the table.

I focus on trying to locate my lungs; somewhere below the neck, I seem to recall. "I'm . . . oh man, I — Hey," I say, made

46

suddenly articulate by the realization that he's just quoted a line from my book, "write your own goddamn dialogue!"

And so. Startled laughter. A beginning. And after an hour or so of conversation, I say, "There's a Newfie expression for how I feel right now: 'man, he didn't know whedder ta shit 'er go blind!'"

The man smiles. "I've heard that too. In England. Or rather in certain parts of England."

I ask him, "Would you like to go for a walk? There's Prince's Island, right nearby. Or we could go to my place, I could show you my own little piece of urban prairie. We could walk my dog."

"Prairie."

"It's what about a third of North America is made of. Gawd, you bloody Brits. You know, I read a Salon.com interview of yours where you told this ridiculous story about football players freezing to death in Yellow Night — "

"What's so ridic — "

"For one thing, it's Yellowknife, not Yellow Night. And for another, it's a preposterous story. Now there was a group of fishermen, or sealers maybe, who froze to death on an ice floe in Newfoundland nearly a hundred years ago. Alastair MacLeod wrote about it in *No Great Mischief*."

"MacLeod?"

"He won the Dublin IMPAC for Christ's sake."

"Yes. Rings a bell, now. You know, I think I should very much like to see this prairie of yours. But I must be back here to catch my limo at six."

"Check out now. You can have a cup of tea at my place, and then I'll drive you to the airport."

47

At my place, the first thing I do is change into jeans and sneakers, while he pokes through the house. I stack a few dishes, check email and voicemail, brush my teeth — you never know — while he makes friends with the dog. I find him in my office, examining the bookshelves. "*The Olympia Reader*," he says. "The Girodias' brothers classics of erotica?"

"Yes?"

"Next to *Ways of Seeing*?"

"Makes sense to me."

He tags along behind me on the narrow path at the off-leash park; the swish of yellowed grass, the spacious prairie sky seem to unsettle him somehow. I'm glad that it's mid afternoon, the neighbours aren't out on the hill with their dogs yet, no need to chat or say hello or worse, do introductions. And the kids won't be home from karate and hockey practice until after we've left for the airport, thank god.

Midway along the slanting path up the hill, he just stops. Dead still. "This is so strange. For years, now, I have had this . . . vision, waking dream, what have you. Of a girl or woman walking before me on a footpath. Sauntering. In a landscape that is strange but also terribly familiar. And this seems to be it — "

I wanted to see the moon rise over the mountain on the last day of August but instead I watch it rise over the city skyline as I walk the dog on the hill. The yellowing grass, Eric yelling up ahead, happy to be reunited with his friends. At least Eric still needs me. I can't keep forgetting the kids! Bummed me out, though, to wake up this morning to the sound of sirens rather than the cry of a loon. And tonight I can't concentrate with Calgary's muffled steady roar, instead of the hooting of owls and the whisper of wind in the trees.

I left Ray a note on the kitchen table at the cabin. And he hasn't contacted me. But I had hot times with the Ray of my dreams last night. His function, perhaps, is to give me hope. And to wean me from Leland. But just now, I glimpse my wrinkled face reflected in the car windows outside the Esso where I suck down a desperate smoke, and the dream dies, all the dreams.

I've developed a bizarre infatuation with REM, I tell my kids.

Matt says he's horrified at such lowbrow tastes.

Eric says, "What's REM?"

A few days ago I dreamed of a fan letter from Leland's real life counterpart, saying that the book I'd written about Leland and Jay had tumbled into his hands. And yes, he passed it along to his agent, to consider a British edition. When I was in grad school, the whole department was madly in love with *Ways of Seeing.* In which, among other things, John Berger asserts that the image of a man speaks about what he can do to you or for you, whereas the image of a woman speaks of what can be done to her or for her.

The fan letter was just a dream. I'm expecting a call or email from Ray, Mister Sunshine. Perhaps my note was too carefully neutral. No, that was just a dream too.

The Leland and Jay scene of his reaction to the suicide is too melodramatic — but it definitely needs to be his daughter, not his wife. And Leland's so flat, a quintessential uppercrust Brit. He needs a quirk; could he be a mimic? Perfect renditions of old falsetto R&B? Country? Tammy Wynette?

Yes, a pitch-perfect rendition of her signature song "D-I-V-O-R-C-E"!

How this bright world that spins in my head bumps up against dailiness. How hungrily I scanned the faculty lounge tonight at that interminable first department meeting. Looking for something, anything, that glimmers with life. But no. The same egos, the same turf wars, the same fortresses of ideology. My colleagues. Everyone in the room looked so old and ugly and tired. And the Department Head giving me the gears about my syllabus for a senior seminar on Gender and Identity in Contemporary Canadian Lit. Why shouldn't I begin with Atwood's early stories? Why shouldn't I end with *The Diviners*? What's he afraid of, anyway? A revolution?

But it's fun to see this department, this campus, as Leland might see it. Because of course he has to come west. After Jay's seen his glittering world, he must try to enter hers. But then he arrives unexpectedly and that's when it disintegrates because by then she's met Gray. Yes, that's good. Because Gray is *of* this place. He's from here, a sculptor. With rough hands.

After the department meeting that refused to end, I phoned Darce. She was just on her way out to hang with her friends. I confessed to some "ups and downs" out at the lake with Matt.

Told her about the bottle pipe, the smell. "I just want to be reassured that it's only cannabis."

Darce chuckled. "I think that's so cute, how you say 'cannabis.' Don't worry about Matt, Mom."

"Well, I can't help but worry. To be honest, he's been a bit of a handful lately."

"Well, I was a bit of a handful at times."

"You were more than a handful, you were awful. But you turned out okay, I guess — "

"You guess, huh?"

And we laughed. The sudden liquid trill of it shook me. When was the last time I laughed? Really laughed?

My dream world has roared back to life. It's Saturday and I am completely out of control. Since I left the Ray of my dreams and returned to Leland, I have replayed the bondage scene in Kensington Suites over and over. Three times Thursday, and last night, god help me, I lay on the couch unable to focus on the World Cup semifinal game, waiting for Matt to leave for hockey tryouts so I could, um, take care of business. Then fine, okay, done, and I sleep, then wake too early but eager for my familiar Saturday pleasures of peace and bed and coffee and crossword. But it pushes in, that scene, the ache (my parts squeeze and swell and ache, dear god) and halfway through the morning crossword I have to stop and run through it one more time and my little boy lies asleep (dear god, I hope he's fast asleep!) in the next room and I'm in the throes and beginning to wonder where is this leading me? where is it going to end? and I have no choice but to get through it but I'm not sure where all this lust is taking me — things to learn, sure, about wanting and dreams and my body and surrender surrender surrender but, dammit —

Leland shows up after a silence of several months in her, Jay's, classroom. He has been mute since the Kensington Suites encounter. But then he shows up, comes home with her, falls instantly asleep in her bed. And I've liked writing him there, trying on Jay's world through his eyes. He's so alien, as if from another planet. But I dread their conversations, I wish they didn't talk at all.

"Sauntering" is the word he uses on the path, the Englishman who inspired my fictional hero, my Leland. We stand amid the dry grass on the hillside at the dog park. "In a landscape that is strange but terribly familiar," he repeats. He looks at me and I look at him. It doesn't seem necessary to say more than that. Because the place where our dreams connect is beyond words.

At the airport, we face each other to say goodbye. I'm beyond nerves now, giddy. I like this man so much, and when the moment comes, without even really thinking about it, I lean close, lay a hand on his cheek while stretching on tiptoe to lightly kiss the other. "You really are wonderful, you know. Way better than the man I dreamed up. I'm so glad. That this happened. That we met. That you arranged for us to meet. Thank you."

He places his hands gently on my shoulders, says, "I fell madly in love with Jay. The loveliest woman I've never met."

I hear the words, but before they can fully register, he says, "Well then," and is gone.

Heart all aflutter when I open the cabin door on a late September Friday afternoon, but there's his note, on the table, *Thanks Janet!* along with his office and cell number and and and *call me anytime, Ray.* It's what I'd hoped for, exactly. It's why I arranged this extra weekend, outside our allotted cottage-time. The pretext is retrieving Dad Moe's pen, which I had found back in August but forgot to pack, and also Eric's warrior staff, which he forgot altogether. I've sent the boys to their dad's, told them I need time to write. I've told no one what I want from Mister Sunshine.

It takes me a while to force myself to call his cell number; an hour and a half of telling myself, "You can do this, you can do this." Imagining every possible scenario, "What? Are you kidding? You're too old and ugly" or "Sorry, can't make it, I'm stuck inside my blonde bimbo of a girlfriend right now, but thanks for calling."

At first, I get his answering machine — very terse: "Leave a message." So I say, "Hi Ray, this is Janet Mair. I'm just here for a couple of days and was wondering whether the water system is all set up now. Could you give me a call, please? Hope to hear from you soon." I figure once I get him on the phone, then maybe, maybe, maybe.

Terribly proud of myself for having made the call, I walk the dog, talk to a deer. Now the time seems to drag though; it's been two and a half hours, and nothing. I don't think I can work tonight; maybe I'll just make dinner and watch one of the movies I brought. Jane Campion's *Portrait of a Lady*, I think.

Saturday morning, and I just spoke to him, just now. Ray. I was very calm. He sounded warm. Like sunshine. He will be here sometime today. Could be a few hours from now or in the evening. That's fine because I am calm now, resigned. And I have a legitimate reason for asking him to come by. Because last night the water system actually broke.

Well. Any time now. I'm powdered and dressed and look about as good as I can. Scenarios suggest themselves but they do not overtake me. The rain pours down from the sky.

I try to puzzle this out, read the signs. What am I doing here? First, numbers were in fact exchanged. I left my friendly note on the kitchen table, just before Eric and I hit the road a month ago. Could have been read as strictly business, or perhaps more: Hi Ray. Please leave your business card so that I can get in touch. I hope the weather clears enough that you can go for a swim! Cheers, J. I left my home phone and email. But. He didn't use them.

Well, at least I didn't scribble *fuck me baby I am so hot for you I could scream*. It's a good thing I was careful, because, horries, Dad Moe has been here for a golf week, and after that he loaned the place to friends of friends, all of whom would have seen the note. But maybe not because of course Ray took my note the day he finished the job, and replaced it with his. So he took my note with him. With my number and email. But then he didn't use them. In the month he's had them.

In the car on the way here, yesterday, I made plans. I'd arrive, I'd call, he'd show up. We'd be naked within an hour. At first I thought I'd prefer to have him arrive at my door Saturday, but then again if it was late Friday, we'd have more time to do all those unspeakable things together we were doing in my head as I drove through the mountains.

So I left him that first voicemail at 3:30 Friday, less than two hours after arrival. Hope faded as the evening wore on and by 9 I had given up. At 10:30 I was in the bathroom brushing my teeth, mouth full of foam, had just flushed the toilet — and there was a loud clunk and the water just stopped. I could hear a beeping noise. Padded out to the basement in my nightie, found the water unit, found the reset button to stop the bloody alarm, but no luck getting the water running again. Had to laugh. How worried I'd been about having no excuse to call Mister Sunshine. And now I really had one.

But what if all that happened was strictly business? In my imagined seduction, he arrives and I am standing at the door. We smile at each other. I say, "Hug or handshake?"

"Hug," he says. But it is brief and awkward. My nipples get hard. He notices and says, "Let's try that again." This hug is longer and the results are, once again, obvious. And then I want to tell him everything, to tell him that no human on earth could be this lonely and not die of it, this empty hopeless place where I've lived so long that any other life seems inconceivable. And how, this summer, something changed. Desire came back. Fiercely. I knew it back in June when I gave a hug to the husband of a good friend, an innocent brotherly sort of hug, and god, I was horrified with myself, but my breasts tingled for a long time afterwards. I was losing my mind. "But then I met you and thought *wow*, I am so far out of step that I don't know what's happening, I mean, I look at you, and you look at me and I feel this energy and I sort of glance over my shoulder and think 'That's nice, wonder what he's looking at?'

And then when I finally decide that it might actually be me, I think 'Oh he's probably a Jehovah's Witness and he just wants me to accept Christ as my personal savior.' Or, this is just a kind of hippie tree-hugger generalized love for all our fellow creatures, and I'm just catching a little piece of it as it goes by."

A lap dance on the couch, rolling and tumbling in the bedroom, me on my knees? Oh my. He mentioned a son who is twenty. So he couldn't be younger than forty. He looks early thirties though. Now as the afternoon wears on I write out these dreamy thoughts, they'll do for Jay in the novel, while awaiting the promised arrival of the man who inspires them; I'm self-conscious, repressed. Can't help looking over my shoulder.

My main character Jay will have to deal with another man, too. With Gray. Who maybe looks a bit like Mister S? Yes, and he discovers her with Leland but then . . . Yes, she can take Leland to the lake so that he can come to truly know her. Then the dinner party. Or the dinner first? Yes, they encounter his place in the world first. Then hers. Whatever order I want. Whatever result I want.

So he arrives, Ray does. With Stan, the guy who looks after the cabins in the off-season. The two of them don't even come to the front door; there goes the hug or handshake. I hear their voices downstairs. I'm rewriting the raunchy section, the one where Leland has her pinned and I'm wondering why I am making this guy use his dick like a weapon. Sure, yeah, sex n' violence R us, but still. I mean, Leland's not such a bad guy, not really. He's an ordinary guy.

My brother's an ordinary guy too. And when he started to become a stranger to me, when we were in our early teens, I used to go rummage around in his room sometimes when he was out, looking for clues. Trying to figure him out. And once I found some drawings he'd made, in pencil. One of them, very lifelike, very well done for a fourteen-year-old, was of a naked woman, lying spread-eagled on her back. A wooden spike was driven deep between her legs. The most shocking thing, really, about this discovery was that I was not shocked. Not then, at age twelve. And not now. It was as if the drawing showed something I suspected anyway, something I'd known all along.

I hear the men working downstairs. Get up from the desk. Rinse my mouth with Scope. Check my hair. Half an hour ago, the daily hello to myself was, oddly enough, a failure. That heat, my constant companion. But today, gone.

I go downstairs to the basement and look at the two men. No acknowledgement. And when I speak? A nice warm greeting from Ray. And then awkwardness. So I say something stupid: "Well I think I'll let you geniuses sort this one out." They both look so insulted. And rightly so. Oh god, there's the rub, the wretched horrid yawning gulf, chasm, between what we imagine and what we actually do. What we actually say. What we hope for and what happens. Dear God. I'm not getting anywhere near Ray today. Stan wasn't in the script, what the hell do I do now?

Well, when the two men come upstairs to announce that they've fixed the water system, I invite Ray to come back for tea, after he drops Stan off at his place. And he does. We talk

57

about kids and music and this festival he went to. Would he like to stay for a beer? For cocktail hour, I call it. And he would. We talk of jobs and travels and friendships.

And after a while, I say, "I've got some chicken I was going to throw on the barbecue. Would you like to stay for dinner?" And he says yes. We eat together, then sit in the living room and he is lovely. He doesn't say anything ignorant or boring the whole evening. We have a few laughs. He stays 'til eleven. Then I walk him out to his car. We look at the stars; he turns to thank me and I rest my hand on the side of his face, kiss his cheek. "I hope I see you again." And again, he says he's around this area a lot. And he jokes that maybe next time I should take a hammer to the water system.

But he never says my name. He doesn't ask me any questions. He isn't particularly curious about me, really. I touch him a couple of times — brush his arm when we sit out on the dock, put an arm around his shoulders when he's doing the dishes. But he is absolutely rigorous about not touching me.

After Ray drives away, I feel like a damn fool. Remove the black underwear, lie in bed stunned. But do sleep, eventually, after two Tylenol. Now I'm awake. Wide awake. It's pitch black out, drizzling as it has all weekend. I listen to my new favourite REM song, "The Great Beyond." The hug went by so fast I can barely remember it, can't even remember what it felt like.

Damn fool.

After he drove off, I wanted to call his cell. *come back. come back. come back.*

But the truth is, as we sat there in the living room, that last hour at least, I could feel my dream slip away; I was tired, I was scared, I didn't think I could do it, I didn't think I could cross that line. This is real. He is a real person. Every gesture, every scenario, every line of dialogue that had played so well in my head just seemed, I don't know, crass. Desperate. Laughable. How do people cross that line? I used to know how to do it, but I guess I've forgotten or the rules have changed or something.

And I didn't come on to him at all either, not really. Well, I touched him, used his name, made some comments (okay guarded ones) to the effect that I thought he was cool. But no. I was way too cautious. I wish I could have told him how beautiful he is.

Here's the end of the story: I got up Sunday morning well before the slightest hint of dawn and walked out onto the deck. The lake and sky were black and silent. I was alone on the planet, and felt so. Couldn't go back to sleep, realized that I hadn't left a key out for the boys for when they come home from their dad's. I didn't want Matt to get home from hockey practice and wreck another window screen trying to break in. So shortly after five on a morning when I could have slept in, I started to pack. Partway through the packing, I let myself cry. A good, redemptive wail out on the deck. (Last night, I told Ray, "I hated it when my boys stopped crying. I'm a great promoter of crying. I think it's good for you," and Ray said, "Oh, they're young yet. Once they get interested in girls, they'll start crying again.") Then I finished packing. Got away around seven. Still dark, but the world beginning to awaken.

Last night, Ray said, "You know a lot of Buddhists say that most of us walk through life asleep." He was talking about the festival where he'd blissfully danced with a completely naked young woman who couldn't have been more than twenty.

Soon as I drove over the creek, onto the secondary road, the fantasies welled up: there'll be a call when I get home, an email. And I had to stop, tell myself *no way, forget it, this is nonsense. Give it up.*

What I want to know is, where's this shit coming from? I mean, for years now, fantasy didn't exist for me. Sometimes I'd lie there at night, trying to summon some sweet dream like the ones that comforted me when I was younger: rapturous scenes of passion, renunciation, romance, heroism, lust, devotion. But the best I could come up with through my forties involved paid bills, decent report cards, maybe the ironing all done and put away. Now I'm overwhelmed by fantasy. It's real life that seems improbable, ridiculous, an irritating distraction. Oh hell, this is mere hormone holocaust, that's the explanation. Last gasp, the insistence of biology. One final blast of estrogen. Or more than that? What then? Does it have something to do with surrender?

That's why I had to revise the rough trade scene at Kensington Suites. Couldn't stand Jay in that first draft — so smug, such a fucking mother hen. She pissed me off. What the hell does she know about what Leland needs, about anything?

Nearly at the highway, it occurred to me that *I* could call *him*. Ray.

I remembered his cell number. By heart.

This past spring, just before this weird surge of lust, I had become forgetful, vague. People were irritated and worried. Darce questioned me about it, and I explained that it was just parts of my brain were fuzzy; for example, I was finishing the daily Scrabblegram in the paper but couldn't add the scores correctly. My daughter said, "Oh okay, I get the analogy. No worries then." Actually, I hadn't been speaking figuratively, but one of the things I love about this kid is that she speaks fluent metaphor. Anyway, the fuzziness passed; not only has desire awakened but also memory. Once again I can look at a phone number once and remember it for days.

By the turnoff onto the main highway, I knew exactly what I wanted to say. At the north end of the canyon, I pulled over at a viewpoint. Checked my wallet, and lo! the note he'd left was in there. And yes, I'd remembered the number correctly. Took several deep breaths. Caved. Said to myself, *You can do this.* Trembled, inside and out. Punched the numbers in but didn't press send. Thought, *This is too hard. I've already been incredibly brave, why should I have to be even braver? I've already phoned him. And invited him for tea. And invited him to stay for a beer. And dinner. I gave him a hug. And a kiss, on the cheek. It's not fair that I have to do this too.*

But it was the only way to end this foolishness. The clock was on 7:40. I made a deal with myself to press send when it flipped to 7:41.

I was rehearsed, expected his voicemail because it was still so early. But he answered. I said, "I was remembering what you said to that cop on the way to that festival. 'Well, if I don't go for it now, I may never get another chance.' So what I'd like to say to you is: I think you are just the most wonderful man, and I wish I had asked you to stay."

A part (a big part) of me hoped that this would make him relieved, and glad. But the truth is, he sounded merely surprised. Surprised, and possibly flattered. Cornered hadn't occurred to me, until he paused and said, "Well. Thank you. That's really nice of you."

"You're welcome. Now go back to sleep." Gawd. Such a mom. Like before he left to drive back to town last night and I'd asked whether he needed to use the bathroom first. God help me, I really did say that.

"Okay," he said. "Well, thanks. I hope I see you again. And you know where to find me."

"Sure. Take it easy."

And even after that, even after that humiliatingly diffident call, I don't know, I tried, but I just couldn't fight it down. Hope welled up, these silly girlish dreams. How strange for reproductive life to end in the same white heat as it began. Only my girlhood dreams were pure romance, rated G. The love theme from *Elvira Madigan*. Rock Hudson and Doris Day, pajama-clad, in twin beds. I did not develop the details, I did not know what's possible.

Jane Campion begins to capture it in *Portrait of a Lady*. Isabel's feverish fantasy on the bed, after Goodwood has touched her face and she has sent him away. (I kept wanting to scream, *Woman, are you out of your fucking mind? That's Viggo Mortensen, for Christ's sake!*) Alone in the room, Isabel replays the moment, but she does not have the physical vocabulary. She dreams caresses, a fully clothed sensual orgy-lite with delicate attentions to her neck and cheeks and waist from all three suitors. She wants passion without really understanding what it is.

So all the way back to the city, scenarios bubbled up, the hope of an unexpected knee trembler on the front porch of my house, but as the evening wore on, I began to let it go, to make peace with it. I'd spent last evening with a lovely, lovely man. I hadn't expected to like him so much. I hadn't really thought about who he was at all. Last night, he made some remark about intuition. I said, joking, "Ah, men don't have intuition, do they?" He argued, said he believed they do, though it's overlooked, disregarded, even dismissed. He said, "I don't want to be a woman. I like being a man."

At eleven, I walked him out to the gate. The sky had cleared a bit, and we looked at the stars. He mentioned sleeping out under the stars just last week, on a camping trip with his daughter. The moment of goodbye came. I touched his face, kissed his cheek. He did not return the embrace.

He is not thinking of me. At all. Whatever possessed me to think he ever was?

Restless that night, woke to cramps, so rare and so random these days that I'd almost forgotten what they signify. Stumbled down the hall, a hot cramp twisting in my low back, a familiar muscular caress. The cramp delivered up dark rich clots at first, a crimson so deep it looked black. And then a gush. A fiery orange gush of blood, a rich bright swirl of colour that mesmerized me, filled me with obscure pride as I stood there, hand poised to flush. It reminded me of a Dabstract, those paint spatter canvasses we made at the

Calgary Stampede when I was a kid. I wish I could have saved
that blood mandala, put it in a cardboard frame and displayed
it on the dresser. I *made* this.

　　Me.

(first draft of)
FINAL DRAFT

The Arts Tonight, CBC Radio

Host: And can you tell me, Leland Mackenzie, how you and Jay McNair first met?

Leland: I was coming in from the airport and heard her voice on the radio, reading from *Richdale,* doing publicity for her appearance at the festival that night. And I thought, "Gawd, that woman writes like a runaway lorry." And the work was so tough, so strong, that of course I pictured this very chunky muscular creature with short-cropped hair and hiking boots.

That night then, there was a reception prior to the reading and I was being herded about and glimpsed this nice little bit of crumpet across the room, thought I might want to chat her up. Never got close, though. So then the reading begins, and my gawd, it's *her.* She's the lorry. This wee thing —

Host: And you, Jay McNair?

Jay: Leland's company delights me. He is never boring. Ever. To have Leland for my companion on the home stretch seems like the most incredible stroke of good luck.

Host: On the home stretch?

65

Jay: The latter part of life, maybe even the last third. And the delight of it is that our characters are now fully formed, we've each become who we were meant to be. And yet, still there's this . . . conversation between us.

Leland: And I'm pleased to say that I am well on my way to establishing myself as a Canadian. Not only can I order a large double double, I can even peel back the little tab so that it latches securely onto the lid. I've learned to remove my shoes at the door, and to say, at the correct moments, "Nice drop pass," and "Through the five-hole."

(Laughter)

Entertainment Canada, CTV: two shot, Jay and Leland.

Interviewer (off camera): So Jay, can you tell us what it was that first drew you to Leland?

Jay: His work, of course. And the fact that he has a really really big . . . vocabulary.

Leland: (squeezes her shoulder, says in a stage whisper *so that's what we're callin' it these days, is it luv?* then turns back to the interviewer) And, of course, what bowled me over about Jay was her nice tight little . . . paragraphs.

Freeze two shot, zoom out to interviewer at news desk, barely suppressing a smile: By all accounts, Ms. McNair, age fifty-four, does have very nice tight little paragraphs. However, the question of Mr. Mackenzie's . . . vocabulary remains a matter of —

Hmm. Maybe not. A bit cutesy. What about this instead . . . ?

FINAL DRAFT

A Novel
by
Janet Mair

She should not think that she was now free. With one
exception, and that was that she was free not to love
him any longer, and to leave him immediately. But if
she did love him, then she was in no wise free.

The Story of O, Pauline Reage

Part One

Toronto Literary Festival

1.

Oh my god, it's him, thinks Jay, at the precise moment that her handler, Laurel, squeals, "Oh my god, is that who I think it is? Let's go introduce you!" and grabs her by the arm.

"No way."

"C'mon, it'll be fun!" Laurel is surprisingly strong for someone who wears size zero.

Jay struggles, protests, "I can't, I'm too — no! Don't you dare, I won't know what the hell to — oh. Hello."

Laurel beams, says, "Leland? Hi, welcome to the festival! I'm from Great North Publishing, we distribute your work here. May I present Jay McNair? Jay is one of our newest writers and we're very proud of her. I'm sure you know her novel *Richdale*?"

He is tall, thin, sort of craggy. Dark hair worn a little too long, rimless glasses, thin face. She didn't think he'd be so tall. He looks harassed yet wretchedly bored, slightly glazed and desperate, but he shakes her hand and says, "So pleased for you. I look forward to reading your work."

"Oh. And I am so . . . I am a serious ad — I'm uh . . . a huge fan."

"Thanks so much. You're very kind."

Jay is now struck dumb. Here she is with one of the most celebrated living authors in the English language and she cannot come up with a single sentence. Well, *I love you* comes most immediately to mind, but somewhere in what's left of her brain a tiny voice whispers *not now*.

He's used to this, obviously. He glances around the room, seeking deliverance from what James Joyce would have called her "confused adoration," but can't seem to find another familiar face. He takes a sip of his drink. He has beautiful hands. Too terrified to continue looking at his face, she decides to follow his hands. The moment stretches into eternity. She looks for Laurel, but she has flitted away. She wants to cry.

"So. Is this your first festival?"

"Yes," she says. "Yes it is. It's quite . . . " She gestures, a limp wave of her arm.

He smiles, though. "Overwhelming? Yes, it is." Nods at someone, takes a step back. "Well, I must — " His voice! No doubt he has already forgotten her name. One more second and he'll be gone.

"You know," she says, "one of my favourite scenes in your work, and I know it's not a major thematic or dramatic scene, of course, but you know how some moments from a novel just really stick? It's the moment in *The Dark* when the central character, the man, is in a little café in a French village, and he's watching a family, and the father begins to mistreat the child — do you know the scene I mean?"

"Yes, I believe I do."

"And the man tries to intervene but his French isn't very good and he goes over to the father and ends up saying something like 'if you touch that child again, I will knock my block off!'"

Leland smiles very slightly. "Yes. How good of you to remember it." Well, what the hell else can he say?

He's turning away, he has seen someone famous and important and not *stupid* — no, not even that, just someone who isn't *her*. But then he stops, asks, "Why do you think you remember it?"

70

"I've never really understood why that is, but I wonder about it sometimes, why we — "

A flurry of bangles and forest green silk and: "Leland! You must meet — oh hello so nice to see you — I'm afraid I must steal him just for a moment."

And he is gone. And she has made an ass of herself. And where the hell is Laurel?

Jay heads for the bar. All around her in the lineup, people are shouting into each other's faces with a noisy social hunger that makes the word *carnivorous* swim into her brain. No one knows her, though. She's a nobody, thank god. She waits in line, and just before her turn comes, a voice behind her, right in her ear, says, "Those moments of transcendence, the felicitous coupling of authorial vision with readerly largesse of spirit, it mystifies me still, how that happens, how that chasm is breached, whether — "

Jay says to the bartender, "That's — white wine please," and to Leland, "You?"

"Whiskey."

"Neat?"

"With ice."

"With ice," she tells the server, and then they wait together, side by side. She says, "I think the scene stuck with me because I once saw some children abusing a dog on a street in a Swiss town. But by the time I'd put together a coherent sentence to get them to stop, they were gone. And it has stayed with me for years. The frustration of it, of not having the words."

The drinks arrive. Stupidly, she picks up both.

"Thanks," Leland says, taking the glass from her. "Such a moment would rankle any writer, I should think. All our eggs are in the verbal basket; how could there be no words?"

"Leland!" A phlegmy male voice, a beefy arm. "Leland, old man, you must join us, someone just made the most outrageous claim about your last book — "

Leland glances at her, whiskey sloshing over his thin white hand. Shrugs.

"No sweat." She smiles. Then leans over and whispers, "Perhaps we can continue this conversation some other time — when you're not quite so famous."

The beefy man tugs Leland away, and she wanders off into the crowd, clutching her glass of white wine, wondering whether he actually talks like that all the time.

She wanders hopelessly in the literary din, smiling a tight, terrified social smile. Risks a glance at her watch — gawd. Only twenty minutes to eight and she has resolutely promised herself that she must stick it out until nine at the very least. The ladies room? A rescue? His voice, behind her again. "What kind of dog?"

"A boxer," she shouts at his retreating back.

Chitchat with a clutch of similarly terrified, vaguely familiar Westerners, equal parts shameful clinging and infuriated marginalization their only common ground. She finally extricates herself, heads to the ladies room. He's just coming out of the men's. "What kind of boxer?" he asks, not slowing down, not breaking stride.

"A brindle!" she yells as he passes.

Front desk 9:05 PM, requesting extra pillows: "Was the dog injured?"

She's getting used to this: "No, I don't think so. It was tied in a doorway. Just one, thanks."

"Messages for 1612? Thanks."

"Tell me, do you believe in sequential conversation? 934. Thanks."

"It has its place. Hard to do at a gathering like this, though."

"No shit, Sherlock."

He laughs. "I beg your pardon?"

"I take it you don't have teenagers. Would you like to go for a drink with me?"

"Actually, I do. Have teenagers, I mean. Yes, I would." He glances toward the piano bar in the lobby. She has not yet had time to panic, says, "Hell, no! Shark tank. There's a place nearby I went to a few years ago — just down the street."

Leland checks his watch. "Let's see. I have to go and be famous for, oh, maybe another twenty minutes or so. Shall I meet you right around here?"

"Sure. No. Outside. Just outside the front doors, d'you see, over there?"

"Right, then." And he's gone, broad bony shoulders moving under a fine wool sports jacket. His hair could use a wash. Jay still hasn't quite registered what she has just done. But she does know that her feet are killing her and guesses that there's plenty of time to go upstairs and change, as well as to ask at the desk for directions to that little place that a friend took her to once, after the book launch last year, what was it called?

The half hour she spends outside the hotel doors are agonizing. Never, in ten years, has she missed smoking so much. But then —

"You're a quick change artist as well, I see."

"My feet were hurting. And I hate pantyhose. Where's your coat?"

"Upstairs. I won't need it."

"This is Canada. You'll need it. I'll wait."

"Yes, Mother," he grins. The ten-minute wait, this time, is pure pleasure.

The bar is packed, but they manage to find a narrow booth in the back and . . . they chat. Pleasant chat about names and ages of children, place of residence, observations about the festival, his panels, interviews, readings, her single reading and radio interview. The subject of spouses is evaded with dexterity; he ducks the question first. Jay has adored this man for years and has fantasized about meeting him, but she can feel the energy draining from the encounter. She senses he's getting bored, and she's perilously close to bored as well. It's only when he returns to the dog that she realizes she has allowed the conversation to flag. "So. It was a brindle?" he says.

"Huh? Oh. Yes. A brindle. Smaller one, a female. Tied up in a doorway. In Neuchatel."

"I know the place. Were you there on holiday?"

"No." She sighs. "And that's at the heart of it, I guess. Because I was there to help my sister. No, first, let me describe the dog. It was tied in a doorway on a residential street, cobblestone, those three or four-storey narrow rowhouses. A group of schoolboys — I didn't have kids of my own then, so

I wasn't very good at judging their ages — but nine or ten, maybe. Anyhow they were pelting this dog with snowballs, close range, laughing and egging each other on. School uniforms — blazers and short pants, little peaked caps, those rectangular satchel briefcases they strap to their backs?"

"Yes, I've seen those."

"It was January and there was a bit of snow in drifts in the gutters. It was a narrow street too. The dog didn't yelp or scream, though. Just stood there shivering with its eyes bulging out, looking so stupid and ugly and helpless. I couldn't even formulate a sentence. *Arret or arreter*? I wasn't sure. *Ca ce n'est pas juste!* No, *juste* is wrong. Or is it? *Vous ne aimez pas si quelque chose* no *quelqu'un* or is it *vous ne l'aimerai* future? Laying a guilt trip is too complicated in French. As I say, they were long gone before I could even collect a few words, and even all these years later, I still can't. Hell, these boys are grown up now, probably have kids of their own, and I still can't, I don't know, forgive myself. Imagine. This happened nearly twenty-five years ago. And besides, I hate boxers."

"Did you write it?"

"Well, I did write a story about that time in my life, but the central image wasn't a dog but a herd of caribou I'd read about, they'd stranded themselves on an island and starved to death for reasons nobody could understand."

"Why were you there? In Neuchatel."

"My younger sister had been at an international school there but she had to withdraw because she was anorexic. I mean, she already was when she arrived, but it got worse over there. It was obvious that she needed to come home and get some treatment so I was the designated family member elected to go over to help, to bring her back home."

"And did you? Help her, I mean."

"Oh. Unlike the dog? Well, I got her home."

He waits.

Jay takes a breath. "She died. In 1985. Heart attack. She was only twenty-three."

Leland is watching her intently, but says nothing.

"So yes, I suppose it's as if — do you think? — the two silences, no not silence, but speechlessness. Are they related in some weird way? You know, the mistreated child in your novel, my abused dog? Hey, why am I answering questions I never even heard you ask?"

He smiles then, a shy smile. "Shall I tell you the story of the moment I became a writer?"

"Yes!"

"I was a wee tad, outside with the bigger kids on a winter's day. I grew up in a little provincial town, east of London. And certainly, a Canadian such as yourself would scoff at my notion of 'winter' but there was, indeed, snow on the ground, and I'd been shoved out of the door by my mother. I was three or perhaps four, swaddled in a canvas snowsuit that made a veritable symphony of scraping and rustling with my every step. And layers of damp scratchy wool, my mittens and muffler stiff with a mix of ice and snot. The local kids were all out sledding on a little hill. I watched this activity with a mixture of dread and fascination. It looked such fun, but it terrified me too. My keeper, a large noisy girl, a neighbour, plunked me down on her sled and stuck her big red face into mine: 'Right then, Leely, want to go down? Shall I ride with

76

you or would you rather go by yourself?' Well, I answered quickly that of course while I should very much like to try it, I was a little bit wary, but perhaps I'd give it a go if she were to sit on the sled behind me like some of the other kids did with their younger brothers and sisters. I pictured myself sort of enclosed in this big puffy cocoon of her arms and legs, and of course she'd do the steering.

"So I told the silly bitch all this very clearly, we had a long conversation about it all, her breathing noise and motherly concern at me, and then? Damned if she didn't plunk me down on the sled, throw the reins at my frozen little mittens and give me a bloody great shove. Down the hill. Alone.

"I thought I would die. I shrieked like a heretic in flames all the way, my screams probably misheard as shouts of joy. I tumbled off near the bottom, having of course not the slightest idea how to make this diabolical contraption do my bidding. Hurtled off the sled and whacked headfirst into a, fortunately, rather small and flexible sapling. A young ash, I believe it was.

"My first thought, on awakening in hospital with eleven sutures in my forehead and a nose mashed to pulp, was 'language is power.' Or something to that effect."

Jay says, "You mean, you tried to tell her you didn't want to go alone, but — "

"But the linguistic capabilities at my disposal then, perfectly adequate for having every need and demand met by my mother, were apparently grossly inadequate in the wide world. I understood that the blame for the accident rested solely with me and I was struck with a dreadful feeling that I could not begin to save myself from wretchedness and pain with the limited tools at my disposal. I became a writer at that moment, as a simple matter of survival." He drains his glass, grins. "Thereby discovering broad new vistas of wretchedness and pain. Another?" he asks.

"Yes," she says. "Do you think, then, that what strikes us as so memorable in the fiction we read is something that echoes or resonates in memories of our own? Or is it a combination of that with some moment of strength or felicity of phrase in the text itself?"

"Not sure — oh, same again please. Thanks. Bit of both, I think. I don't know. I'm always amazed with what people read into my work, the things they remember, the things that strike the average reader. And of course the way that the stuff I've made up out of the whole cloth tends to be the stuff people regard as the most 'true,' the most autobiographical."

"Me too," she says. "Isn't that weird?"

"Though I must say, these days, people — I mean ordinary readers, not critics, not people in the trade, not fans or sycophants — but ordinary people who just read for pleasure — well, those types don't seem to say much to me anymore. Or if they do, I don't hear them say it. I forgot what I was going to say — "

"There you go," says the waitress.

"Oh that'll be lovely, thanks." He waits a moment, then leans forward. "Why do Canadians say, 'There you go'?"

"Do we?"

"All the time. It's the oddest thing . . . " He turns to her with mischief in his eyes. "You examine me, Ms. McNair."

She startles, flushes, then gets the tease, and grins back: "If you're going to quote Charlotte Bronte to me, pal, you have to give the rest of the line."

Now it's Leland's turn to flush slightly. He clears his throat: "You examine me, Ms. McNair. Do you find me handsome?"

"No."

"No, *sir.*"

"Right. No, sir." *Liarliarliar!* "But listen. I just had an idea. There's something I'd like to give you."

He cocks his head, says silkily, "Really? What might that be?"

"Oh god, don't come on like that. It doesn't suit you at all."

"It doesn't?"

"No. It's . . . unseemly." She likes him so much already that she doesn't even mind the flash of dismay on his face at this. "Let me give you a gift. A reading of your work. Let me be your ordinary reader. And I really am. Yes, I teach first year English, and yes I'm a writer, but in terms of your work, I'm just an ordinary reader. Because Canlit is my teaching area — not to mention my national literature, and also, in the crassest professional terms, the competition — I read it differently than stuff I read for pleasure. So I don't know your work except as a pleasure. I read very little American fiction; all that manly bluster and wrestling with the Big Questions of Life. Which all too often seem related to securing the adoration of a nubile younger woman. I read a lot of contemporary Canlit of course. But I read English writers for pleasure. Not to be well read or literate, but simply for enjoyment. I read women, mostly: Drabble, Byatt, Barker. But in terms of male Brit Lit your books are the ones I . . . remember, I guess. The ones that stick. So. Will you let me do this? Just tell you what I liked and what I thought and felt, and what I found striking?"

Leland regards her for a long moment, considering. Clears his throat. "If you like," he says.

"Okay then. Ground rules. You must keep completely silent. No reactions, no questions, interjections, corrections. No writhing in agony when I get it wrong, even dead wrong; no slapping yourself upside the head for your failure to communicate adequately, and especially, especially, no slapping me upside the head screaming, 'No, no, no, you twit, good god woman, are all you colonials bloody illiterate?'"

His sudden laugh is throaty and unreserved.

A surprise. It takes him a moment to catch his breath, then he says, "All right. Agreed."

Now that it's too late, it occurs to Jay that this is a dreadful risk. She knows nothing about this man: she knows him intimately . . . but what the hell. She's sitting in a bar with a Booker prize-winner that she's had a crush on for years. Her, Jay McNair, a nobody, a Western Canadian, a single mother, a part time college lecturer; what the hell does she have to lose?

"So. The big names in male Brit Lit are . . . yourself, of course. Then there's, well let's just call him the curmudgeon with father issues. I honestly think I've read more *about* him that I have of his actual work and the few shorter pieces I've gotten through are just so self-consciously tragic and dark. Anyway, so I start this big bloody novel of his that a good friend has raved about — isn't it awful, I can't even remember the title, not *The Corrections*, that was the American guy who snubbed Oprah, bless his heart — "

Leland raises his hand.

"No! Not a word, remember? But the book was just . . . nasty. Well written, witty, virtuoso even. But the characters were

80

nasty, the narrator was nasty. And worst of all was this sort of self-conscious brilliance in the writing. Writing that kept jumping off the page and going, *Did you see that? wasn't that amazing?* Frankly, it irritated the hell out of me, and I closed the book after about twenty pages and muttered, 'Oh shut the fuck up, you smug prick.' Did I say chortling was allowed? I guess I'll just have to let it go.

"And then there's the other big name — let's call him the erudite postmodernist. I really liked him. Now, admittedly it was in grad school that I read him, and of course I thought his deconstructions of literary norms were absolutely brilliant — clever, inventive, hilarious. But you know what? If you ask me now, ten years later, to remember one single detail of these books, I could not do it. I can't recall a single detail of plot, or anything about a central character, not even a line of dialogue or an image. Nothing. And to me, a truly good novel cannot be forgettable in that way. It has to stick. It has to bear some kind of truth that you can carry away from it. So really, yes the erudite postmodern is an entertainment, a lark. A really good one night stand, so to speak. But not a relationship. Not a romance.

"So we come to you. That was just the preamble. Are you ready? Don't answer, just nod. Okay. The first book of yours that I read, a long time ago, was *Theft of Love*. What you really got at, for me, was how that kind of pain and unknowing is so utterly unbearable that it just rips you apart. I think there was some kind of supernatural or metaphysical aspect to the couple's final coming back together after their loss — maybe something like Jane hearing Rochester's voice through the window at the moment she's about to succumb to Rivers. I don't remember precise details but I do remember the moment. I don't know whether the novel actually suggested that they'd come back together to make another baby. Perhaps I was just left with the hope that they would.

"Next, *The Dark*. Scene of the older man present at the dismantling of the Berlin wall, this potent combination of the personal and the political. And the woman, I remember, had inherited a farmhouse in France. Her family had obtained it for next to nothing from people who'd been forced out by the Nazis. So the impression I kept from what I read then is a sense of the burden of history, I guess. Of how we all live our little lives ignorant of, no not ignorant, but forgetting or trying to forget how social and historical forces have shaped us. How powerful and important the past is. And of course there's the scene in the café, the man's frustration in wanting to do the right thing, to help this little kid, and not being able to find words.

"*Perchance to Sleep* came next, I think. One bit I remember very clearly, a paragraph I read and reread: just an offhand remark by one of the central characters at a social event — a wedding or funeral — and he asks himself, 'How did we all get so rich, so comfortable, so prosperous without ever really noticing or thinking about it?' I liked that line so much I actually copied it into my commonplace book — "

"You have a — "

"Shush. Yes, I do. I'm a closet Victorian, I guess. Anyhow, the part I remember most vividly is when the guy is out on the moors, trying to seduce his Muse, and at the moment she comes to him, and he's seized with the passion of creation, the intense wonderful moment when inspiration flows through him, he is presented with a moral dilemma, a choice. And he chooses with hideous but shamefully recognizable egocentrism, to continue composing.

"How'm I doin' so far? Don't answer! At least you're neither weeping nor cringing, and you appear to have all the hair you started out with this evening, so . . . now for a truly embarrassing confession. I haven't read the one that was just made into a major motion picture. Well, you know how it is, so many books, so little time. But I loved the one before that, *Regret*. Particularly the bit where the young couple are having a knee trembler, and the young guy is wanting to hold back, and is filling his mind with thoughts of wastebaskets and rubber boots. Priceless, and something I'd entirely forgotten about young men, poor things. So . . . I guess that's it. I'm done."

Leland looks at his hands, then directly at her. Says nothing for quite a long time. Then, very quietly, "I think there's a little more. Isn't there?"

Elation tumbles into terror. He knows she's lying. Jesus, why didn't she think this through before she opened her fat yap, Christ almighty —

"Okay. Okay, I was less than honest. Okay. Shit, I can't believe I'm doing this. I did buy . . . you know, that major motion picture one, of course. In hardcover. And started it and found it very rich. And stately and detailed. Reminded me of *To the Lighthouse*, that loving, devoted attention to time and place and class and family dynamic. You know, I think it was probably my own time and place that interfered, my own family dynamic; I was in a tight spot, a really frantic spot, at that point in my life, the details of which are unimportant. So I set the book aside. I knew I couldn't give it the right kind of attention at that moment. You know that yourself, I'm sure. You have to be receptive to a book, and at that moment I couldn't be. I hope to be, though. Some day."

He sits back now, appears satisfied with the addendum.

She says, "So. That's it. Was that okay?"

He hems, smiles slightly, and reaches over, very lightly encircling her wrist with his fingers, then just as quickly withdraws them. "You're tiny, your wrist is so small, yet your hands look like they belong on someone else. Someone much larger."

Jay regards her hands with interest and dismay. The knuckles reddish purple and flaked with dead skin, fingers thick, nails unpolished and raggedly manicured with a toenail clipper, thumb pads cracked and dry — not bleeding yet but they will be by winter. Raised purple veins on the backs of the hands, palms blotched red, nails sprouting little colonies of torn skin along the cuticle. She is mesmerized by these ugly hands of hers and can think of no way to reply, so the two of them sit in silence. He too seems disinclined to speak and finally she murmurs, "Well. It's getting late."

It's as if her voice has wakened him: "Yes, right. Of course. Here, let me — " and he's left the table in search of the waitress and their bill.

She can't decide whether to beat herself up now or later for doing such a stupid presumptuous thing. Giving Leland Mackenzie her dimwitted response to his work, and going on and on like that, Jesus, who does she think she is? He returns to the table, though, with an air of brisk cheerfulness, and they set out back to the hotel. She is talked out, emptied. Scared. And it is her, not him, who lapses into silence as they walk.

84

Leland, very gently and with practised decorum, asks a few tactful questions about her schedule tomorrow, the weather, her future writing projects. Slowly she is able to slide back into her normal social self, responding as if on autopilot. A sense of loss consumes her. This night, this amazing night, all those foolish things she planned to say, never mind the foolish things she actually did say — oh yes, she has been writing this scene two or three pages ahead while living the present, an occupational hazard; she has already pictured herself in the elevator, saying, "This has been the most amazing first date, not that this is a date or anything, but I have had so many disastrous first . . . encounters that — " and then off into her hilarious stories about the African grad student and the recently bereaved husband and oh yes the famous poet — unless she gets Leland into her room, but wouldn't they have stopped talking by then?

The loss she feels is more than disappointment. This isn't the deletion of a good scene. It's that she opened to him, in that little bar. She could think out loud in his presence — Charlotte Bronte's phrase "audible thinking" occurs to her — and he, Leland . . . received her, she knows he did, she felt it. The gates opened, but now they are closed. She thinks he closed them, but she's not entirely sure. There was the caress —

All gone now, and they are walking side by side, chatting up a nervous storm, and she will never get to say it: *This was amazing, you are amazing,* and her heart feels broken. The lobby lights are far too bright and harsh laughter booms from the piano bar. "Are you — ?" He stops midsentence and gestures toward the crowd at the bar.

"Gawd, no! Drunk writers at this time of night? Spare me."

"I think I'll give it a miss as well."

The elevator door stands open and they step inside. Jay punches the nine, but he makes no move. "What floor?" she says.

"Oh. Um . . . 12. No, sorry. 16."

She presses the button and they rise in silence until the chime sounds at the ninth and the doors open.

"Well," she says.

"This was a — most pleasant evening," he says.

"Yes. It was. Well. Good night."

She shuts the door of 934 behind her and leans against it for several minutes, eyes closed. For some reason, she's thinking about Anne Lamott's memoir. How Lamott talks about different kinds of prayer, describes a friend of hers whose morning prayer consisted of the word "whatever" and whose night-time prayer was "oh well."

"Oh well," Jay murmurs, and gets ready for bed.

2.

Leland stands in the elevator, watching the doors *whush* closed, hearing the chimes ring, feeling the floor rise under his feet. He remains perfectly still. At 16, the machine waits politely for him to make up his mind, and when he doesn't, the doors *whush* closed, and the elevator carries him back down to the lobby. He stumbles toward the roar of noise from the bar but catches himself at the entrance and pauses, listening. *I have known them all already, known them all* — the high shrieks of laughter from the women, the boozy bravado roars of the men. He does a pirouette and shortly finds himself back in the quiet of his suite, pouring a glass of whiskey over the few remaining slivers of ice.

He can't believe this. No invoice, no bill. He cringed from the moment he took her funny rough hand in his, to the moment the door slid shut behind her: what will it be? what will this cost? A blurb at the very least. The name of a really good agent. Maybe a little help with chapter four, or maybe a quick read of the whole manuscript, no rush, just when he has a minute. A famous fuck, of course. That's a given. And he liked her so much. And is actually grateful for the last truth of what she said. She'd been so there, so righteous, so unshakably real that he'd seen immediately that when it came to the novel she hadn't read to the end, she had lied. He knew that, and it shook him, thrilled him, because he'd felt for some time now that he couldn't tell anymore, couldn't tell whether the work was good or not, couldn't tell whether people meant what they said. Anyone — lovers, editors, total strangers. And it occurs to him that for years now he has coped with this gradual blindness by simply assuming that everyone lied. About everything. All the time.

But with Jay, he could tell the lie and he called her on it, and she came through. As far as she dared, at least. And he liked her so much and was so grateful that he just couldn't face the rest of it. Receiving her bill.

But it never came. How could she not want anything? He pours another glass and paces. He can't figure this out. Flicks on the TV and quickly turns it off again. Sits at his laptop but does not raise his hands to the keyboard. Contemplates the phone. Pours a third drink, then has an idea, and heads down to the bar, with a stop at the front desk on the way, to arrange for the bellman to come to his door next morning at 6:45 precisely for the message he is going to write:

Midnight: First Draft: *Sorry for being such a constipated shit last night, but*

3:00 AM: Second Draft: *I really enjoyed our talk last night and was wondering whether*

3:10 AM: Third Draft: *I can't believe you haven't read what half the world thinks is my best book you daft twit*

6:40 AM: Fourth (and final) Draft: *Hi Jay: Want to meet at that same bar again this evening, around 10:30 or so? LM*

3.

She arrives at 10:20, hoping to have time to reapply her lipstick and maybe brush her teeth. His reading tonight was very good, and the crowd adored him. Her radio interview in the morning seemed to go okay, and when she called Calgary, the kids were fine. Well, at least the house was still standing, or so they said. But all that day, that note that note that note, oh how it buoyed her up —

But there he is already, how in hell did he escape the mob? The line at the book table ran right out of the hall and into the lobby —

"Well, then," he says and gestures at the seat across from him.

His imperious tone frees her to insist, "Back in a flash, just have to make a pit stop."

Her face in the mirror — dread, anticipation, delight. And oh if she could just stop these ridiculous fantasies, these romantic scenarios, *You know what I really wish? I wish that I could be given a chance to learn to love you. And he smiles and pats the place beside him —*

Back at the booth, and he smirks, "Pit stop? No shit Sherlock? You're providing me with quite an education, Jay."

"Well. There you go."

He grins. "The usual?"

"Yes, please. But are you sure you're up for this? I heard that you had to cancel your gig on the international panel because you have the flu."

"A lie. Never felt better. Spent the day in bed, reading."

"You're not ill?"

"Not at all. Listen, I read the most wonderful book today; it's called *Richdale* and I want to give its author the gift of a reading. From an ordinary reader. A fan."

"Oh god."

"Rules: you are to remain completely silent. No protests, no blushing, no — "

"You've forgotten the first rule. The author has to agree to hear the reading."

"And do you?"

"No!"

He takes her hand as the waitress brings her white wine, and his, what, second whiskey?

"It would be such an honour for me to do this, Jay."

She has to look down, his eyes are, dear god, she's going to, god only knows, cryfaintscreampassout?

"Jay?"

"Just give me a minute." He won't let go of her hand. His touch is gentle but strong. His thumb moves over her knuckles, exactly the way her father used to, holding her hand when she was a little girl. Safe. A breath, a deep one. Then another. "Okay," she says.

"Good. *Richdale*. What struck me the most. The promise of that little town is inextricable from despair. It made me think that possibly the two are inseparable. The graveyard with the single stone, the solitary Mary, the ghost of every lost or discarded child. Very good. And the bit at the end where Sally re-visits the houses, photographing them as a way of attesting to their reality. And then finding the new graves. It would have been far too neat to have exactly the right number; excellent that you didn't fall into that trap, that temptation.

90

"But that scene — *the* scene, okay? — in the little coffee shop in the town near the homestead, the man with bright blue eyes, Jamie's bastard son, now a grandfather, spooning pudding into *his* granddaughter's mouth, looking up, recognizing something in Sally. Lovely. They can't meet each other's eyes; it's a sad moment but somehow deeply funny as well."

Jay can't look at him. He gets it, he got it. Her ideal reader, the person she wrote this book for, the consciousness she wanted to address, awaken, touch.

He adds, "I plan to reread, of course. Pick up whatever I missed, on the plane home tomorrow. I need to think more about how the dispossessed, the exiled, have this absence in their histories. My own ancestors were far from rich, but they had their place in the world and they chose to keep it. But Sal's forebears, like yours I guess, had to begin again. Or chose to. And what a gift that choice was, yet what a burden too. I know where every one of my ancestors is buried. Every house inhabited by a family member still stands, the churches and the schools and the pubs. But with your lot, the past is erased over and over again, with each push west. And yet Sal and the others need to go back anyway, digging in the bloody soil with their bare hands. Sal's moment in that valley, as if the landscape itself is recognized as her first mother. It goes far deeper than any such I've ever read, man or woman."

Jay's mouth is parched. Her gums crackle when she opens her mouth to drink.

He watches her, a shy smile. "You may speak now, if you wish."

Don't go. don't go home.

91

"Or not." He looks slightly anxious, grabs his glass and drinks.

Hands. That's it. Something to do with hands. Jay covers his hands with her own, mutters, "Not that this is a date or anything."

"Pardon?"

She lifts her hands. "I realize that this isn't what I'm supposed to be talking about at this moment, but for some weird reason, I want to tell you about the worst date I ever had. It was with a poet. Older guy, quite well known. We'd met at a conference in France. And though we'd said goodbye at the last session, we ended up on the same train the next morning, both headed for Paris, he for a long stay in a borrowed apartment, and me just overnight before my flight home. He asked me out for dinner.

"I was so excited about this. A famous poet, a romantic evening in Paris. And it was such a fucking disaster. For a variety of reasons, but one was that he saw me as this, I don't know, cushion or something. Munro has a line about 'undifferentiating welcome' when she describes a mildly retarded girl at school who is sexually used by the boys. That's precisely what this man seemed to expect from me, to want me for: undifferentiating welcome. He seemed surprised that I didn't know his work, but did not say anything or ask anything about mine. He basically *performed* the whole date. Really. It was as if he was the performance and I was supposed to be the adoring audience, beaming, gasping, applauding. Every move, from the inside story on the Cambodian waiter who served us aperitif at the sidewalk cafe in St. Germain, to the carefully selected cosy little bistro and, 'May I take the liberty of ordering for both of us?' to the after-dinner stroll down to the Seine, the big finale on the Pont Neuf with Notre Dame illuminated in the background, where the music swells and she falls into his arms and and and . . . But I swear, Leland, by the time we got to the violin part, I was so goddamn furious, so insulted by his condescension and his complete lack of interest in me or my work or my opinions — hell, an inflatable doll would have served his purposes just as well, better — that I very deliberately said, 'Nice view. Hey, I have to get going. Can you show me where to find a taxi?' And yes, there were a variety of things I was pissed off about, but a big one was that in that whole evening — can you imagine spending an entire evening with anyone, say from 6:30 'til nearly midnight, and not asking one question about that person's life or interests?"

Jay sips her wine, and goes on: "What happened afterwards, though, was what cut it for me. Because I went home, and after I'd cooled off a bit, I went to the library, not the bookstore, mind you, the library, and took out several volumes of his poetry. Because if you meet a person who is a writer and you want to . . . respect or know that person, then you read their work. And then I sent him a polite note of thanks, on email, for the dinner, and made some comment on his work. And then I waited for some word from him. He knew I was a writer, my publications were listed on my bio for the conference, and he could have given the slightest indication that he knew I was a writer too. But no. His reply was, if possible, even more arrogant than his behavior in Paris. It was one of those email replies where the person just returns the sender's email with his own responses inserted between the paragraphs, or even sometimes the sentences. Lazy as hell for one thing, and insultingly like receiving a graded undergrad paper back for another. I sent no reply and haven't heard from him since."

Leland begins to speak, but she raises her hand to stop him. She needs to take a moment to assemble the last fragments of thought.

"So. I can't seem to find the right words for how I feel about what you've said. Not flattered, that's servile. So is honoured, as if some higher being has deigned to give my work his attention. I mean, I know that my work is not me, but it's a bloody important part of me. I can't find any word that explains how your reading — which by the way is absolutely dead wrong on every friggin' count — how this reading..."

He waits, alert now.

Again she places her farmwife hands over his, simply covers his fine white hands with her own. "Thank you."

"You're welcome."

"And how did you manage to get the book so late last night?"

"I was heroic. I braved the madding crowd at the bar downstairs, found that silly heavyset woman with the big square glasses and browbeat and pleaded and bloody well had to offer to marry the silly bitch before she'd take me into the storeroom where they lock up the book tables for the night. Read 'til three or so, then slept a few hours 'til it was time to send you the message — "

"Valued, maybe that's the word."

"Possibly. Read again straight through with a couple of calls to cancel things. I knew I couldn't get out of my mainstage reading, of course, but all the rest of it — "

"Believed in?"

"Cherished, maybe. So I got a few people irritated, but a bloke can only do what he can do, and the flu defense was airtight and I figured that the world would probably go on today without another wise and witty encounter with The Author. Now, finding your first book has posed a larger challenge, I'm afraid — "

"Publisher sold, distributor broke."

"But I'm on track and expect to have it in my hands for the flight home tomorrow."

Home. Tomorrow.

"Recognized, perhaps," she muses.

"Or: beheld."

"Beheld. I like that. Munro uses that word in 'White Dump'."

"Can I get you folks another round?"

Home. Tomorrow. "I don't want you to leave. Oh fuck, did I say that out loud?"

"Yes, I believe you did. Yes, same again, thanks."

4.

It's after midnight, and Leland and Jay are walking back to the hotel. The wind is vicious, icy, and he has tucked her arm through his. He wants to tell her why, to explain his silence last night, his withdrawal, but he guesses she already knows. What he does say though is, "You were so honest with me last night, but I could tell when you backed off, when you did not speak the truth."

Jay says nothing.

"And once I'd had the chance to — well, I'd got the pip, certainly — but past that, I suspected that you hadn't finished the book because it lacked precisely those qualities that 'stuck' (to use your quaint, rather ignorant colonial expression) — "

"Screw you, ponce."

"How the things that you remember have, for lack of a better word, a heart — something human, something recognizable. And what I have suspected for some time now is that that is precisely my own misgiving about that particular book; I fear that it is mere technique. I didn't love it with all my heart the way I did the others. I see it now as an . . . exercise. I did it to see if I could."

"I didn't mean — "

"Shut up. I'm being truthful and disarmingly, dare I say Canadianly, 'open and honest.' Disgusting phrase, makes me think of Nixon and encounter groups at the same time, god help me. Besides, what you meant does not matter a whit, because what I received from your completely incompetent prevarication was a treasure, really. Of having to face this feeling of being . . . emptied out. It is my greatest fear, always has been. Of using it up, you know."

They walk on in silence, then she mutters, "So I've mindfucked the greatest living novelist to the point of despair? Dandy."

"You give me far too much credit. Women always do — "

She grabs his arm, stops him, makes him face her. "Don't call me 'women'!"

"Pardon?"

"Don't lump me with 'women.' I hate that."

"You're a woman, aren't you?"

"Yes, but I'm sure as hell not 'women.' Especially said like that."

"Fine. All right. Shut the hell up and let me thank you, most seriously and sincerely and with a bloody big lump in my throat, for telling me something so blindingly obvious about myself that only the biggest twit in the world, namely me, could fail to notice it."

"You're welcome. And you know why I hate 'women'? My husband used to send me postcards from all over the world, before we were married and after. And he'd always begin them with 'women.' As in, "Hi women, miss you like crazy, having a wonderful time, the weather is great!' Really. Every letter or postcard I ever got from the guy, he misspelled 'woman' and wrote 'women.' And, in the end, I discovered that it was a spelling mistake that really signified, if you know what I mean."

They're in the elevator now. "Speaking of linguistic freight, Jay, I am hoping very much that you'll invite me in. To your room, I mean. I am speaking quite literally here. No touch of figuration whatsoever, I assure you."

"Well, it's too late for me to say I don't care whether you leave or not."

"I believe it is."

"So I'd better invite you in so that we can continue the conversation. Of course bearing in mind that we are both mature and sensible adults."

"Practically senile — "

"No Hollywood scenes."

"Agreed. D'you think we could still order room service?" he says. "I'm a little peckish."

5.

Jay shrugs off her coat and stands paging through the hotel directory at the desk. She sees him, in the mirror, come up behind her, looking over her shoulder. "Just chips and popcorn at this hour, I think. But I did see a pizza menu somewhere, here — "

Leland has moved close; she can feel his whiskey breath on her cheek. He hasn't touched her yet — oh god — he places his hands, palms really, on her hips. There could not be a more accurate place to begin — well, except for, oh, right *there* — his lips brush the skin of her neck just below the hairline, lightly at first then more assuredly. Jay, goddamn her, swoons; a shudder shakes her shoulders and a small exhalation escapes her lips. He murmurs, "Hmm, that's a good spot." Pulls her against him, still touching that exquisitely hungry spot inside each hip and she can't, she just —

"Hey." She spins around to face him, drapes her arms over his shoulders and kisses him on the mouth, fervently, with a simultaneous rip of terror. Just as he responds, she pulls away —

"Okay. Look. Umm. I have to — Oh shit. I can't do this."

She finds herself hiding in the bathroom, sitting on the edge of the tub, head in hands. Cowers, shakes, tries to gulp air into her lungs. She doesn't know how long it takes for the sound of her heart pounding in her ears to ebb, so that she can hear the expectant silence in the room out there. And then his voice. His lovely voice. Propelled by her body, not her thought, she flings open the bathroom door to confront him, sees him standing by the desk.

"Leland, I haven't been with a man for . . . a long time and I'm — "

He looks at her, the phone in his hand. "How long is long? Yes, 9 — what's the room number?"

"934. Years. And you must understand — "

"934. Do you mean to tell me you haven't had sex for years? No, not *you*. Or do you mean, just not with a man. No, *definitely* not *you*. Of course not. I'm so glad to hear that. Double pepperoni, yes, thanks. 934, yes." And hangs up. "May I ask why?"

Jay fidgets, can't meet his eyes. "It's kind of an accident."

He doesn't laugh, or smile. He just stands completely still, asks softly, "What do you want me to do?"

She spreads her hands in front of her, as if breaking up a fight between two toddlers and says, "Okay. Listen. Don't leave. I need to . . . go back in there for a minute. But I don't want you to leave. Okay?"

"Don't. Leave. All right, I think I've got that."

"I want you to stay."

"Yes."

She crosses the threshold into the bathroom, but pops back out again, peering around the door. "Take off, oh let's see, no more than . . . five items of clothing. That includes shoes. And wait for me right there in that chair." She points to the easy chair next to the bed.

"Is five a maximum?"

"For now."

"One more question."

"What, for god's sake?"

"Two shoes make one pair, right?"

100

"No! Two shoes is two items. Remember not to leave."

Safe inside. Thank god she has left her nightie and robe on the bathroom hook. It's the customary flannel tent, Bay bargain basement, thick fluffy cotton, chin to wrists to ankles.

She is trembling all over. She pees, washes her hands, fluffs her hair, brushes her teeth, uses mouthwash, washes the makeup off her skin, briefly considers then rejects the notion of reapplying it, and instead (what if he leaves?) performs her usual routine of Lancome eye cream and Renaud wrinkle defense. A sprinkle of baby powder under the arms . . . how long has she been in here? Perhaps he's still out there. There's nothing else she can do. She must open the door, she must. She can't.

6.

Leland watches her emerge from the bathroom, swaddled in layers of cotton and velour, already talking, explaining, "It was an accident, okay? Maybe an evil witch put a spell on me. Maybe I just kind of forgot to be attracted to men for a few years." She is near tears.

He knows that he must not approach her, must not touch her. Not yet. "Okay," he says. "It's okay."

"I want you to stay here with me tonight."

"I will."

"It's a crazy idea — "

"No it isn't. Look, why don't you hop in and I'll just sit here — "

Trembling, she nods and, keeping her distance, crawls over from the far side, scrambling under the covers. Once she is in the bed, he moves to the chair, draws it close and puts his feet up on the edge of the bed, not touching her outstretched legs, but close to them.

"Here's a question," he says. "Worst Hollywood bedroom scene ever?"

"Glenn Close and Michael Douglas in *Fatal Attraction*. The kitchen sink thing. And the stewed rabbit. Oh take the other sock off, for Christ's sake."

"So six is okay."

"Socks count as one. A pair of socks."

"Inconsistent. And dead wrong. Kathleen Turner and William Hurt in *Body Heat*."

"Are you crazy? That was so hot. How about Jessica Lange and Jack Nicholson in *The Postman Always Rings Twice*?"

"'Rip me, Frank!' The original was better."

"Not available in the provinces. Blockbuster had a lock on entertainment where I come from."

"Lana Turner and . . . I forget who else. Never mind, what about best love scenes? Susan Sarandon cleaning off the clam juice with lemons in *Atlantic City*?"

"Oh yes. And *Bull Durham*? I recommended that movie to a friend going on a first date. She didn't speak to me for a month."

"All time, though? Miranda Richardson and Rupert Everett against a wall in *Dance With a Stranger*."

Jay closes her eyes, then — "Oh yeah. Yes, I remember that one. You could very well be right. For once."

The pizza arrives, and Leland carries it to the bed, flopping down beside her, and opening the box on his lap. "I hope you like pepperoni and mushroom."

"I hate mushrooms, but I can pick them off."

"My elder daughter, Katie, used to do that too. Pick off the mushrooms, but then she'd arrange them in a neat little pyramid and eat them after the pizza. Dessert I guess. That's when she still ate."

"Oh. Oh dear."

"Yes, the affliction, like your sister. Well. We've managed to get her into a good treatment program, though. Making progress now."

"I'm glad. How long?"

"Six months now? Oh, the anorexia? Set in at about fifteen, which is the norm, I guess. A refusal. The willful blindness, it's maddening."

Jay says, "I once forced my sister to pose for a photo beside me. The two of us in bikinis. See? This is normal, on the right. And on the left — "

"Greyish skin stretched over bones, spinal column exposed. The intent is control, and the effect is so dreadfully ... vulnerable."

"I'm sorry to hear this, Leland. It must make your heart ache."

He carefully takes away the pizza carton and napkins, sets them on the coffee table, says over his shoulder, "You should get some sleep. Scrunch down."

"Oh lord, that's what a gynecologist says before a pelvic. Or maybe it's scoot down."

"Then lie down, for Christ's sake." He crosses the room. "Here, lift up," and lies down beside her, on top of the blankets, sliding an arm underneath her neck.

"Mm. Did I mention I don't want you to leave?"

"I won't. Sleep."

"And you won't leave."

"No. I won't."

To his surprise, and probably hers too, he feels her body relax, hears her breathing slow. He leans over and whispers, "Remember how that feels, when the children were little, this little body growing heavier in your arms."

"Yes. I loved that."

He watches her drift deeper then gets up to remove the rest of his clothes. As he crawls back into the bed, she reacts sleepily but vaguely.

She murmurs, "You know, Carol Shields has a scene like this in *Happenstance*."

"I know her work, but I don't believe I've read that one."

"Just like this, a chaste embrace. Way more polite though. No swearing. And the man is wearing pajamas."

He thinks about that for a moment, then whispers, "Fuck that shit" in her ear. She laughs and snuggles back against him. He pulls her close. Lets his thigh graze the back of her leg, his mouth brushing her neck, hand resting close to her chest. She finds the hand and brings it to her lips, then lets it go again. Hours, minutes? He feels himself growing hard against her, but doesn't want to move away. Eventually, the problem is obvious, and he mutters, "Er . . . um. Just ignore that."

She is still. He waits. A full beat.

She says, "Ignore *what*?" Laughs, then, and wriggles back to meet him.

7.

"Injury accident on the 401, the Gardiner very slow as well," crackles from the clock radio next to the bed. A nudge. "Hey, look who's back."

6:45. Jay arches away. "No way, I don't do mornings. A morning hard-on is pure mechanics anyway, seventy percent blood flow, thirty percent needing a leak. I could be a loaf of Wonder Bread and you'd be just as turned on. Besides, we both stink." She throws open the covers and jumps out of bed.

When she emerges from the bathroom, he's ready in line, looking disreputable and rather sly. She's back in bed when he returns to the room.

"I have to go. An interview."

"It's tough to be famous. Don't you still have the imaginary flu?"

"Can't get out of this; it's by phone, to London. Go back to sleep," a kiss, "and I'll order us some breakfast."

"Up there, where the suites are? Are the unfamous even allowed on that floor?"

He pulls away, and she is bereft. The lonely years, touch-starved eternities of endless nights, seem pallid and small compared to this; she keeps her back turned as he gathers his clothing. "Go ahead, turn the light on," she says, but stays where she is, resisting the urge to snuggle back into the place still warm from his body.

She says, not looking at him, "You know what's really amazing about all this? I slept with you. I mean, as in sleeping. I thought I could never do that again. I mean, even before, I nearly fell asleep. That really tells you something, don't you think?"

"That I'm incredibly soporific?"

"No! My last affair before this long . . . um, drought, was with a man I met in a coffee shop. He was a salesman for an office supply company. We arranged a dirty weekend together, at a hotel in the mountains. And as usual, the sex was great; this man had a growth at the base of his penis that looked hideous, like a squashed pink prune, but it worked just like a French tickler."

"Jay, it is entirely obvious to me that you haven't been getting out much in recent years or you'd recall the basic etiquette that a lady doesn't discuss previous paramours while her man is still trying to find his bloody socks — "

"So that he can get the hell out of here."

He stops, belt in hand. "I must. But I'll call room service, order us breakfast in, oh, two hours or so? What do you usually have for breakfast?"

"Two prunes and a banana." His grin prompts her to add, "I am being completely literal here."

"Right. And tea?"

"Coffee. Intravenously if possible. When do you want me?"

"Around nine, I think. You really are lovely, you know?" Grabs his jacket and tie and strides out the door as she curls up around her naked self between the sheets and just smiles.

8.

"So this is how the other half lives. My god, flat screen TV. And a balcony. Cream no sugar. Thanks. So," she takes the cup from him, and sinks into an easy chair, "you've made your calls then?"

"Yes. Now tell me please, in excruciating detail, about all the other men you've ever slept with."

"As in sleeping, not screwing?"

"As in the man with the prune — "

She looks at him, a question hanging in the air between them, but shrugs it off.

"Okay. The man with the prune. Afterwards, we lay there in this hotel room bed, all night; I listened for his every move, his every breath, prayed he'd fall asleep so I could get out of bed and just, I don't know, go to the bathroom, fart, just be away from him for a minute. And oh, every rustle of the sheets, and this dreadful tinkly new-age dreck and the glow of the screen — we had left the TV on for a soundtrack — I swear it was the longest night of my life. Anyway, an hour or so into the ordeal, I realized that he was wide awake too, tensed, waiting for *me* to fall asleep, probably for exactly the same reason. And I decided then and there that I would never again share a bed with someone I didn't love."

They both let that comment settle a moment, but she holds his gaze, resolute.

He asks, "That was the last time?"

"Yes. But listen, the weird thing is that, oh twenty years before, the best sleep I ever had was with a man I didn't love. He was Dutch, an artist. Not a lover. A painter. Long story. Communal living arrangement in the early 70s . . . nuff said?"

"Sure."

"So one night, I was alone in my room in the Dorm. This was the building where encounter group participants were housed, but we were between groups at that point."

"You mean the *you do your thing and I do my thing* sort of — "

"Yes, Fritz Perls and Jung, eastern mysticism, all that. So this man, Theo, was the lover of the wife of the man who founded the centre. Oh hell, everybody was sleeping with everybody else and I guess there'd been a big blowup in the main house that night, because Theo got really drunk. He drank a lot less than the rest of us, usually, because he wanted to be able to paint. I knew squat about art then — "

"Squat?"

"Nothing."

"I'm going to need a dictionary."

"I didn't understand anything about art at that point. Actually I still don't, but anyway, I knew that these . . . things he painted, he called them masks, these twisted tortured, splattered human faces leaking off the edge of his canvases, I knew I felt these images in my chest. Does that make sense?"

"Bacon's paintings did that to me from the first look," Leland says.

"Yes, I know him, the screaming popes. So Theo. Well, that night I could hear him ki-aying outside, but I drifted off, and then before I knew it he's in my room. He forgets his English when he's drunk, so he stumbles in babbling in Dutch and just collapses on the bed beside me and passes right out. He has this dog, Boris, a big snarly Shepherd, very protective and scary, who grunts down at the foot of the bed. I realize

I have to pee but I know if I set foot on the floor, Boris will take my leg off, so I cross my legs and go back to sleep. And in the morning, there's all this drama. Irene — the woman Theo is having an affair with, the wife of the guy who runs the encounter groups — she comes into the room. I open my eyes and she's just standing there at the foot of the bed, staring. Says not one word. Of course, Boris doesn't growl at her. I don't actually know whether Theo has taken his clothes off. I always slept naked then. But Theo's still out cold — "

"Your virtue, such as it was, remained intact?"

"Yes, definitely. Bit of a snuggle perhaps, but what I'm trying to get to is the sleep. With Theo beside me, I had the most amazing dreams I can ever remember. Colours I couldn't have even imagined, swirling faces, everything liquid and shimmering, sparkling. Another world, or a glimpse of it."

He regards her in silence, sipping his tea. "Ah. And?"

"And. Last night was like that. Not colours but . . . I can't describe it. I mean, here I am in bed with somebody Really Bloody Famous, not to mention a serious hunk, and I fall asleep. And when I did there were these . . . not colours, though."

"Not reams of bloody print, I hope?"

"No. Stories. Adventures. Around every corner, something amazing, wonderful. But way more important was, you know how in dreams you're always trying to say, trying to tell, and either you can't get the words out or there's just this soundless scream?"

"Yes, I know it well. I dream it all the time," he says.

"But last night, Leland, not that you were there in the dream, but . . . I don't know. I just knew I had someone to *tell*. I just felt it. What did you dream?"

He takes his time. Too long. But she waits.

"A dream I often have," he says slowly. "Watching a girl walk through a field. Saunter, actually. She has a dog with her. I dream it again and again. I don't know why. The place seems familiar, but I know I have never actually been there, I'm sure of that." He falls silent, rubs his eyes.

Jay takes a deep breath, asks, "How was the phone interview?"

"Fine," he says. Warily.

"And I expect you also had to make some calls."

"Yes," he breathes.

She sips, hesitates, then asks, very softly, "Who did you call?"

"My agent."

"And?"

" . . . Home."

"Coward."

"My wife, then."

"Ah," she says, "of course."

Silence.

He shifts in his chair. Sets down his cup. "I dreamt, also, about a house in the country. It looks Georgian — sweeping grand double staircase up to a landing, where a woman waits for me. Welcoming me. She's holding back a dog, by the collar. Sometimes I'm walking up to the staircase, sometimes I get out of my car. Last night I remember getting out of my car. It's late, the woman is in her nightdress, but she welcomes me

111

anyway. We do not know each other well, but I have asked to come to her and she has agreed. My call woke her up but now she's waiting for me at the top of the stairs, holding back her dog. I go up the left side of the staircase, and she introduces me to the dog, gentles it, and then invites me inside."

"And?"

"I never see what happens after I cross the threshold."

She does not speak.

"You must have known, Jay. Don't play the wounded innocent."

"I read your work, dipstick, not the literary gossip in the *Times*. We don't get the *Times* out in the colonies, you know."

"You read author bios. You know damn well. Come on, it's the first thing anyone ever looks at. The blurbs, the synopsis, then the bio, the dedication."

"Yes, of course. Because it does matter who is speaking. Okay, I'm a coward. I knew. Not as a fact, mind you, but as a supposition, and I chose not to ask. I'll tell you something, though: it's a truly classy man who can show interest in a woman and at the same time let her know he's married. I met a man like that, once."

"Another man? For a celibate, you really — "

"He was a roofer, dammit. About ten years ago. I was freshly abandoned with two kids and no money. I had put my house on the market, but every time it rained, the roof leaked, water in puddles all over the place during the Open House. Desperate is too mild a word to describe me at that point. Beleaguered, hopeless. And this kind blue-eyed roofer came to fix the skylight. He noticed some loose shingles while he was up there, so he offered to come back the next day, a Saturday, at no extra charge, but I didn't believe it for a moment. And then Saturday morning comes, I'm in bed reading the paper while the kids watch cartoons, and I hear this truck pull up, the clank of a ladder outside my window, open the shade in time to see his shins moving up out of view. By the time he comes down, I'm dressed and about as presentable as I can get at that stage of my life, which isn't very, and we sit out on my front porch with coffee and a smoke. Did I say he had blue eyes? Oh yes. And a kind smile and slim hips in his torn jeans, longish hair. And only minutes into our conversation, he mentions his wife. Lovingly, respectfully. As a given, a pleasant fact of his life: 'My wife says' and 'my wife does the books,' that sort of thing. So there he is, with me, for me, doing me a practical kindness as well as the intangible kindness of noticing that I am a woman, somewhat attractive. Or at least with a reasonable shot at being attractive again some day. He knew I was alone, I knew he was married, and we just sat together peacefully on the porch for a while. A mutual salute. I thanked him, and he said, 'You're welcome,' and he drove away in his truck and I never saw him again."

Leland looks distracted, obviously thinking it over, then asks the question: "Who will *you* tell?"

She is momentarily confused, then gets it. "About this?"

"Yes. About this."

"Who will you tell?"

"No one."

"Why should I be any different?"

"You told me about the roofer, didn't you? And the painter, and the man with the prune. Do you think the roofer told his wife, by the way?"

113

"No idea. But he might have. No. Probably not. But he could have. Are you thinking I'm going to broadcast a famous fuck or something?"

"I have no idea. Are you?"

"If you have to ask that question, you don't know me at all."

"How well do I know you, Jay? In situations like this, I can't predict."

"Situations. Plural."

He takes a breath. "I'm in a difficult position. I've been threatened, blackmailed, extorted — the tabloids in Britain are scum, absolutely vicious, and it seems that almost everyone has a price, if not the woman herself, then some acquaintance. It's just so fraught, this — "

"*This* meaning every time you fuck some woman at a festival?" The coffee cup misses his temple by a millimeter, but the contents splatter in his hair, drip down his glasses. "I assure you, dickhead, that I am not one of your fucking situations!" The saucer follows, but she bobbles it like a Frisbee, and it barely clips his shoulder before ricocheting into the dresser. "I am not a *this*. I'm not *women* either. You got that?"

He removes his glasses, wiping off the cold coffee. "I intended no repartee. It was a blunder!"

Furious, she throws her hands in the air, hisses, "So you can quote Bronte *in extremis*, fuck you anyhow!" and moves to the door, but stops there and turns back. "Listen. About the same time as the roofer, I happened to walk past the television one night, on my way to tuck the kids in. You were being interviewed on the evening news. The sound was off, and there was no lettering along the bottom of the screen saying your name. And I saw your face on the screen and I stopped dead still. My breath caught and my heart fluttered and I thought, oh. Oh, he's lovely. Just *you*, not the author, not . . . anything. Just you. No doubt you don't believe this story and, frankly, I don't give a flying fuck whether you do or not, you dumb prick. There, that's my salute. Take that back to London with you."

9.

Jay walks along the quay for a long time. She tries not to hope that he is out looking for her, tries not to think that he might have filled her room with flowers and abject notes. She walks for nearly three hours. She knows his plane is at two, so she figures he'll have to leave for the airport no later than noon. Oh, wouldn't it be romantic if he missed his plane for her, wrapped her in his arms in tearful apology, swearing his love, their new life together beginning right at this moment . . . so shameful, these hopes of hers.

12:45. No messages at the front desk. 12:50. No voice mail, no flowers. No notes. She's a damn fool.

She undresses, lies motionless and dry-eyed on the rumpled sheets for another hour, then another. When she is certain that British Airways has departed for London (she goes online to check), only then does she allow herself to cry. By four, she rises, makes herself presentable and takes a cab to her cousin's. The evening passes in a noisy daze; the cousin's polite questions about the festival quickly give way to the din of the children's demands, and the truly startling news that another child is on the way, due in late spring.

She calls another cab as soon as she decently can, but it's nearly ten before she makes her escape. As the taxi approaches the hotel, she is rummaging for her wallet, with one eye on the meter, but then the façade of the bar — their bar, hers and Leland's — catches her eye.

"Stop here, please!" she says, and pays the driver and walks back the long block. She is beyond hope, beyond caring whether it's acceptable for a woman her age to walk into a bar alone on a Saturday night. Their table is occupied by a group of Asian teenagers in wifebeaters and blond-streaked hair, but the one behind it —

"Hello." Leland acknowledges her curtly, and without surprise. He signals the waitress, who brings Jay's white wine and his whiskey as he speaks: "My wife's name is Christa. She's German, a ceramic artist. We have our son, now ten, and her daughter, fifteen. My two older kids visit on school holidays. Christa is ten years younger than me. We met at a gallery opening of a mutual friend. She is a fine woman. Kind, attractive."

Jay takes a moment to absorb this information, then says, "She doesn't compete with you."

"She is supportive but not ambitious. Not for the same things, at least. Are you just coming from that dinner at your, was it a cousin? Tell me one hilarious thing that happened to you today."

"This has been a day singularly devoid of hilarity," she says. "You go first, then maybe I'll think of something."

"Right then. So there I was thinking 'she's gone, *that* was a blunder indeed,' and trying to rinse the coffee out of my hair, and arrange it to conceal the bruise on my temple, when I get a call from a producer who's in town from Montreal and wants to 'talk some serious rights' on my work. I say the usual, 'Sounds interesting but I have a flight to catch, get in touch with my agent,' but this guy, his name is Larry, absolutely insists, saying, 'I gotcha covahed, don't sweat it.' So I have spent the day with this funny little gnome of a man. In a limo and he's throwing wads of cash around — metaphorical cash but the numbers are big huge ones, the kind that make a modest Englishman positively blush. One expression of his I

117

just loved was 'Ya got DAT right, pal!' I miss my plane, but he arranges a spot on his company Learjet, leaving tonight, just before curfew at Pearson." Leland glances at his watch. "So I've got about ten more minutes."

"Did you sign anything?"

"God no. But it gave me this chance. I thought you might come back here, tonight."

They watch each other, now. Closely.

Jay takes a breath and begins: "I lied. Too. I will tell one person. My closest friend. But I will swear her to secrecy. We've been keeping each other's secrets for nearly thirty years."

He slides out of the booth and opens his arms. "Come here."

Jay scrambles out of her seat and nestles against him. "We should be careful. We're in public."

"Fuck the public," he mutters, nuzzling her neck 'til she pulls away.

"Wait! I just thought of one funny thing. I called home from my cousin's place, just to check in. I've got my son Ben, who's seventeen, looking after his little brother Danny this weekend. And so Ben picks up the phone, says hello, and I hear what sounds like a very large party in the background, and clear as a bell, a voice right next to the phone yells, 'Ask 'er if she wants ta suck my cock!' It's Ben's best friend. And my very rebellious and normally articulate son gets all huffy and embarrassed and hisses, 'It's my *mom!*'

"It took every ounce of self control I had not to laugh, to pretend I hadn't heard. And I swear, the next time I see that buddy of his slouching through our front door and we do the usual chitchat — *how's school? any luck with that part time*

118

job? — all I will be hearing in my head is *Hey how'd ya like to suck my cock?"*

It's a chilly night in October when Jay and Leland say goodbye, laughing together, for what they both believe is the last time.

10.

From: lcMackenzie@hotmail.com
To: "Jay McNair" jmcnair@telus.net
Sent: November 12, 12:10AM
Subject: query
How'd ya like to suck my cock?

_____

Reply:
From: jmcnair@telus.net
To: lcMackenzie@hotmail.com
Sent: November 13, 8:00AM
Subject: dream on
See subject heading
p.s. how did you get my email address?

_____

Reply:
From: lcMackenzie@hotmail.com
To: jmcnair@telus.net
Sent: November 13, 12:10AM
Subject: next question
Are you sure?
p.s. got my agent to call your publisher, saying I'd read
your work and wanted to congratulate you. They supplied said
address with shameful alacrity.

_____

Reply:
From: jmcnair@telus.net
To: lcMackenzie@hotmail.com
Sent: November 14, 8:15AM
Subject: get over yourself, you arrogant prick

120

Positive.

p.s. did you read that piece in the *Guardian* about Harold Pinter's cancer diagnosis? How sad.

It was Jay who asked for the first phone call, frustrated with trying to discuss the latest act of atrocious stupidity of George Bush in writing, so he called, and then he called again, the time change a bit awkward, but her supper hour in Calgary on Wednesday nights when the kids were with their dad coincided quite well with Leland's mid-morning tea in London.

And Jay began to live for those calls. Until one day, in the midst of a heated debate about the lapse of powers evident in the latest Atwood, he said, "Oh. Hold on a moment, will you?" And she heard a woman's voice. And then Leland's voice responding. In a kindly and reassuring tone, yet also a little impatient, a little dismissive. She heard a door close, then the rustle of the phone held against his chest as he listened (probably) for his wife's retreating footsteps. He seemed to listen for a long time.

"Sorry, a literary luncheon in the works, but plenty of time, really. So what were you saying about the scene in the garden?"

"Leland." She is humiliated. "Oh. I can't do this."

She hears his sigh. No words.

She says, "I have to go. Bye."

"I understand," is all he says.

A month passes before he emails again; she reads his cautious but deliberately provocative comments on the recent Byatt/Drabble scuffle, and her reply to his closing question

121

forms in her mind the moment she stops reading. But no. It's a trap. She hits the reply button, then send. Shoots him a blank. He will know that she has received his message, but that she chooses to be silent. And it ends. All of it.

Part Two

Six Months Later: Literary Gathering at the Savoy in London

11.

Jay, stunned and terrified, is being shepherded through the crowd, introduced to shockingly famous people by her handler, Shin Joy, a stunning and unterrified young woman with a tuft of vertical maroon hair.

Sheer vertiginous dread — is he here? Even deeper is the dread that he isn't.

She stands to one side of the stage as she is introduced. She has never, in her life, been so scared. She has never felt so small. Over the years, she has learned to master this terror — the shallow breathing, the shaking hands, the pounding heart and red flush to the face. She has learned not to resist it or be scared of it, but just to let it come in the hours and minutes leading up to the performance, and then to let a sense of surrender take over. People have told her that she seems completely calm and relaxed on stage. She just smiles.

"It is my great pleasure to introduce — "

Applause. Her legs feel rubbery, knees won't bend. She gulps for air, her mouth so dry that her lips stick to her gums. A good trick is to admit the nervousness, publicly confess it and thus make it human, but words desert her completely. She's not going to make it, she can't do this —

"Thanks so much . . . " (name a blank) "for that . . . kind. Introduction." Voice shaky and pitiful and thin. Even the tiniest drop of spit would be enough, just a single — "I'd just like to do a short, um . . . " Breathe, dammit! "Reading from the. Um, first ch — "

"Pardon me."

That voice.

"I'm so sorry to interrupt but — " The rush of feeling at the sound of that warm kind voice — "but I'm not sure that we'll be able to hear you properly in the back."

he-ah you prawpawly

"So if you wouldn't mind just — "

She is suffused then, a feeling radiates out from the centre of her chest and to every extremity, the trembling stills, blood moves through her again, her mouth moistens. She moves the microphone down so that it aims at the point of her chin — something he taught her back in Toronto. "Is this better? Okay, then. Perhaps I should begin again."

She has learned from watching Leland read to select two or three vivid, short sections, all of which leave the listener wanting to know more. To end with warm thanks and a polite statement to the effect that, "I don't wish to take questions. I do thank you all very much for honouring my work with your presence and attention this evening. I look forward to speaking with you out in the lobby in a few moments."

In the hubbub following the reading, she can tell she's in London. The wineglasses aren't just glass (Toronto) as opposed to plastic (Calgary), but they appear to be fine crystal. The appetizers actually look appetizing, no mangled curled-up cheese on a Safeway tray, but uniformed waiters passing silver platters laden with smoked salmon, shrimp, samosas with mango chutney. She scans the room, trying to remember how to make polite conversation while tracking, tracking; he wouldn't just leave, he couldn't. She is introduced to a plump, sweaty little man with a thick grey moustache, streaked yellow under the nostrils. And only after their brief, stilted conversation is over does she recall where she's seen his name before: on the masthead of the TLS, Jesus Christ almighty, but there —

Shin Joy cries, "Oh Leland. How lovely to see you here. May I present Jay McNair?"

His kind grey eyes, grave smile, his cool smooth hand. "We've met, actually. Last year, I believe it was. At the Toronto festival."

"Yes. Yes, Mr. MacKenzie, it's . . . good to see you again. You're looking well."

He has held on to her hand just a fraction of a second too long. He's still *there*, but cautious. "Enjoyed the reading very much. Has no one offered you a glass of wine?"

Shin Joy slaps her forehead. "My god, I forgot. Leland?"

"Nothing for me, thanks. But I promise to guard your precious charge 'til you return, and to introduce her to anybody who's even remotely important."

"Bless you," Shin Joy trills and negotiates her thin body with lithe expertise through the crowd.

Because of the noise, Jay has to lean close; what is he saying?

A voice bawls in her ear: "Mizz McLean, what a pleasure to meet you, I so enjoyed your reading, and . . . why Leland, what a surprise to see you here, you never attend this sort of thing!"

By the time she has corrected this over-made-up inter-loper — "it's McNair, actually" — and been introduced to the woman's under-made-up companion, and then the compan-ion's agent, and then the agent's neurasthenic and infuriat-ingly gender-nonspecific escort, the space where Leland stood has been reoccupied by Shin Joy, bearing wine.

The roar of sound in the room suddenly seems distant, muffled. Jay sleepwalks through an exchange with the extremely intense editor of a famous feminist press; she knows she should be paying attention, but can't focus. She abruptly excuses herself, ignoring Shin Joy's squeals of protest, and bolts for the lobby, eyes down but senses alert for his presence.

She huddles in the bathroom cubicle for as long as she dares, then rouses herself to face the din for a few minutes more — twenty, tops, before she can escape for good, pleading jet lag. He's not in the Thames Foyer. Not near the door. She tries to move purposefully through the room (she can sense him), figuring that if she just keeps moving, she'll see that blue-grey tweed shoulder, the sweep of greying dark hair. He's a tease, always on the edge of her admittedly myopic vision, then disappearing again. She finds herself trapped in a clutch of near hysterical Canadian expats all screaming at once about the oil sands and the Stanley Cup, one of those cross-purpose conversations where she observes her social self as if from above, as if she's having a near death experience; oh god, sees herself and her companions shouting at each other as if they are wild beasts arguing over a kill —

"Excuse me, I believe you dropped this." His hand. A matchbook. He drops it into her pocket.

"Oh thanks, I — " but he's gone.

She manages, in less than two minutes, to extricate herself from the expats, but the journey from there to the exit is a minefield of must-meets and do-say-hello-tos: it is nearly 9:45 when, gasping, she achieves the front doors of the Foyer, moving quickly outside into the April evening. In the shadows of the marble columns, she snatches up the matchbook. The Red Lion, a pub, an address, and scrawled inside, *10:30?*

Crowded, smoky — he wouldn't be at the bar. She notices small anterooms towards the back, she thinks they might be called snugs, and fights through the crowd. London seems like one big crowd after another, suffocating. He's there, in the last little room at the back. She slides eagerly toward him on the faded brocade banquette, but a slight recoil, a tightening in his shoulders, warns her off, sets the limits. This is his hometown, people know him here. "Can't you bloody ignorant Canucks tell time? It's only ten past."

"Can't you snotty Brits be a little flexible for a change? You saved me out there in the — I was going to say 'arena' because that's what it felt like."

"My first impulse was to shout out, *breathe you silly bitch!* But I opted for something a bit more subtle."

"Well, it worked. God, I haven't frozen up like that for years."

He sits back, sips his drink. "I found it rather amusing. Especially because you certainly know how to freeze a guy out."

She looks at him with what she hopes is insouciance, but underneath the table, her left hand is tightly holding on to her right, to keep it from drifting onto his thigh.

"Six months," he mutters.

"Yes."

"Come on. No word. No attempt."

"You have a wife."

"You expected me tonight."

"Did I?"

"You reacted to my voice."

"Maybe." She turns the conversation to the surface of things, the vagaries of literary travel. When he brings the second round of drinks, though, she says, "That's something I always thought that Charlotte Bronte got wrong in *Jane Eyre*. The scene with the gypsy? She would have known it was Rochester as soon as she heard his voice."

"No. I think not."

"You just said yourself — "

"Jane could have had no physical sense of Rochester," Leland says quietly, reasonably. "Neither she nor her creator had sexual experience of any kind. You and I, though — "

"Bullshit! Leland, you of all people should know it all happens up here." She points to her forehead. "This woman wrote the most perfect romance of all time. Well, along with her even less 'experienced' sister. I'm saying it's an authorial mistake, not her lack of experience. *Jane* would have known him at once, because *Charlotte* had done the most unspeakable things with Rochester in her cold little bed in the parsonage in Haworth, night after night after night."

"As you have with me? Before we ever met, I mean."

"Perhaps."

"Am I even better up here?" he grins, tapping his head.

"No comment."

"Well, you're fabulous in my head. You're always on your knees . . . "

"Oh fuck off."

"So. How are all your little cocksuckers these days, anyway?"

129

"What?!" She startles, then gets it. "Oh." And the exchange of news — kids, work, gossip — carries them until the lights flash and the bartender announces time. Leland does not hesitate: "Can I come back to the hotel with you? The family's in France. I join them there tomorrow."

"Well, then — "

"I'll just pop into the gent's — "

But when she glances around the partition, she sees him standing at the end of the bar, his back hunched, a telephone held to his ear.

The heavy door of her room clicks shut behind them and she is on him with a hunger that she observes with a kind of detached dismay. She has him undressed within minutes, but then leads him to her bed and makes him wait there while she prepares herself in the bathroom, wriggling into a lacy ensemble purchased for just this eventuality. She makes her entrance only to find him watching the late news on TV but he genially switches off the remote, pronounces her outfit "very alluring" and tugs on the lace straps so that it billows to the floor beside the bed, lying there 'til morning.

"This is the BBC world news. The EU Council of Ministers will meet in Brussels today to discuss — "

"Jesus Christ," Leland groans, reaching over her to fumble for the OFF button.

Jay says, "I had to. I've got an interview, have to get ready. And you have to go anyway. Don't you?"

"Come here."

130

She twists away, raising her arms to drop the discarded nightie over her shoulders. As it floats onto her body, she says, "They're not in France, are they?"

Silence.

"Not exactly."

Silence.

"We're all flying out together. This afternoon."

"What did you tell her when you phoned her from the pub? No, wait, don't tell me, I'm sorry I asked."

"We've got a little more time, Jay. Here's your chance to fulfill that deep-seated, most secret desire of yours — " He reclines like a pharaoh, nodding slightly crotchward, a devilish smile.

"You're out of your mind," she says. "I have to go be famous now, well, moderately famous, and you have to find your clothes."

She notices that despite her puffy eyes and ratty hair and probable toad breath, she feels absolutely ravishing today.

Leland appears to concede, wriggles out of the bed. "Right then, I'll be off." But stops with his boxers drawn only half way up, another smile and gesture, "Though I'm sure you've changed your mind — "

"Trust me on this one, sunshine. I've never been so sure of anything." She waits 'til he is safely dressed, before she can risk the admission: "When you made that call last night. At the pub. I knew. I really knew this time. And I decided not to care."

"Was that difficult?"

"It was made easier by the fact that this time I'm, well, being dishonest too. No, I'm not married, but I've been sort of . . . keeping company with a man for a few months now. His name is Gray. A sculptor. Someone I've known and liked for a long time, and things just — "

Leland twists in his chair, tugs his shirt collar, turns his back to her. At last he asks, in a cool voice, "Is he good to you?"

"Yes, he's interesting and fine and kind. And single. When I'm with him, I'm happy."

He looks away, as does she. Then he crosses the room and disappears into the loo, closing the door softly behind him.

She sits in the easy chair he has just vacated — blissful, stupefyingly sad. This could be the last time. She's crazy, she's lost, isn't even aware that he's returned to the room 'til he crouches before her, gently lifts her hands, taking each one, first the right, then the left, to his lips. She tries to see his eyes. "Leland. When I'm with Gray I always wish I was with you."

"I wish I were."

"You uppity prick."

"Well, then."

"Yes."

"I'm off, then. To France. And you're off to spend a famous day."

"And afterward a couple of tourist days. I've got a friend covering my classes the rest of the week."

"Well, then."

He hesitates, then says, "Last night, I did an experiment, actually. Before the reading, and again after. I tracked you through the room. It was odd, really. I tried not to speak, but on occasion, just to preserve what miniscule social reputation I still have left in this town, I did have to respond verbally to someone. And you reacted to my voice from a distance of about three meters. I could see your head turn, you were trying to locate a familiar sound. Amazing, in all that din. Your other sense, though, your bodily sense, was not as . . . well it was acute in the sense that your reaction was more visceral. There were several occasions when I passed close by, always at your back though, and I could see your senses heighten, a kind of animal alertness visible in the way you held yourself. It had to be closer than for the voice, though. A metre or so. I found it rather erotic."

There's nothing more to say. He rises, knees creaking. She rises too, and leads him to the door. She turns the knob, then looks back to see him standing motionless two paces behind her.

A slight gesture to a place just below his belt buckle. "Last chance," he says. A wicked smile.

She takes a deep breath. "Son of a bitch!"

She whirls, grabs his shirt front and pulls him toward her, then shoves him back against the closed door. Pressing his chest firmly with one hand, she runs the other down his shirt front to his belt. Realizing quickly that the operation will require two hands from here on, she eases her thighs and hips against him to hold him still, arches back (all those years of doing Cobra in yoga class paying off big time) and undoes the belt and trousers, backing off only to let his shorts fall like cottonwood fluff in June. The shirt-tails are an obstacle, so after some caresses of his hips and backside, she unbuttons the shirt from the bottom up, ending with a tender kiss at the base of his throat. His eyes are on her, but she will not meet them; she's not interested in anything above the neck. He doesn't speak, and she bats his hands away when he reaches for her,

133

one hand sweeping his chest and nipples, the other moving on his nascent hard-on. She sinks to her knees.

Jay has often thought it an odd fact of her historico-cultural moment that she learned how to give head a full year before her first full sexual encounter. She obtained the information from a book on her parents' nightstand, a paperback bestseller called *The Sensuous Woman*. At fifteen, she pored over this book with biblical fervour, memorizing the Butterfly Flick, taking to heart the suggestion to "lightly flick his testicles (balls) with your free hand." To this point she has been fairly neutral on blow jobs; in fact once, in her early twenties, a combination of too much booze and poor depth perception caused her to gag and puke all over a guy's belly. But now, today, this moment, she is liking it very much indeed. She thanks the anonymous author of the book now, most fondly. Leland is liking it too. His whimper of pleasure, his surrender to her hands and mouth seem the sweetest things on earth. He's close now — she's been using one hand at the base, and the other to flick and cradle away, but now he's very close, and she takes all of him into her mouth, moving her hands on his butt and thighs, and massaging his hips with her thumbs. He gasps and cries out and then slumps against the door, his breath ragged yet deep. She holds him in her mouth a moment then gently releases him. She remembers that "the recently depleted member must not be handled roughly." So she slides up to her feet, wet mouth on his belly and chest and throat, then begins to dress him. Top shirt button first, down to the bottom, then crouching to pull up his shorts, ever so tenderly tucking the little soldier, still bobbing, inside. She crouches again to retrieve the pants, and aside from an occasional oops

134

from her, and a gasp from him, they are silent. The button on his fly gives her some grief, as does the belt — one usually does this from the other side — but she manages, gently tucks the shirt in, rests her hand on his chest, smoothing the shirt front with wifely propriety. At last she meets his eyes. They're deep and wild, but she feels perfectly in control, blissful, relinquished. She pats his chest. "There you go," she says. Then steps back, and in one smooth motion, twists the doorknob, hands him his jacket, and shoves him out the door, shutting it behind him.

12.

Leland stands, stunned, against the door, blinking in the sudden shocking brightness. He can't remember where his legs are, or what they're for, so he stays completely still, head tilted back against the solid surface, eyes closed. He really is quite disinclined to move, and in the remote area of his brain capable of coherent thought at this moment, he senses that Jay waits silently on the other side of the door, listening. But what more is there to be done or said, really? More of the same guilty chances. Sure, she knows about Christa, and the children. But not about Christa's episodes. Nor about Meg.

"Excuse me, sir. Are you unwell? May I be of any assistance?"

Bellhop. Christ almighty — "Fine, really. No worries." Leland detaches himself from the door, staggering slightly with the sudden movement. "Sorry." Did he hear a rustle of silk behind the door, an intake of breath?

"May I help you find your room, sir? Have you forgotten your key?"

"No, I'm not a guest, actually." Christ! And as he is propelling himself toward the elevators, who should he pass but the gossip columnist for the bloody *Mail*? Jesus Christ, worse luck, dammit, dammit, dammit — "Yes, lovely to see you, too. I'm just — uh, good day!"

But outside, the April morning shines brightly in the wet streets and Leland observes, as if for the first time, how richly colourful the world is: the flowers in pots outside the hotel, the cheery jackets of passersby, the reds and blues and greens. He hails a cab for the train station and home.

13.

Another six months pass. Jay nearly misses his name in a mid-October flurry of department email. Her students appear to be suffering from every form of disaster the human imagination can conjure: dead grandma, sick grampa, snowed in, roommate trouble, spouse walked out, even a couple of pregnant pets. It takes her a moment to see it, to register his name. And the single word on the subject line erases any hesitation.

Subject: please
Something terrible has happened. please come to me in London as soon as you can. Love, Leland

First essays are due back in a week. Midterm scheduled for Friday. Mom in hospital. Hockey, soccer, dog, kids. Her first response is "Why?" She deletes that and begins to write "Okay but you must tell me — " She paces. Deletes that too. Her third attempt begins "Okay, I'll see what I can do — " but stops there. She paces, makes half a dozen phone calls, then writes and sends:

Reply:
Subject: yes
AC 496 arriving Thurs 19th at 3:14. Love, Jay.

He's not there, at Heathrow, when she arrives, rumpled and sweaty. Instead, a cheery little man with bad teeth and a grey uniform stands with a cardboard sign that bears her name. The driver takes her bags and shepherds her to a limo idling in a Strictly No Parking zone.

Once in the car, she ventures, "Is Mr. Mackenzie all right?"

The driver growls, "A family tragedy, no doubt. At least they've kept it out of the papers." After an hour in traffic, they pull up to a two-storey building on a quiet street; a small discreet sign announces Kensington Suites. Glass doors slide open to admit them. At the front desk, a handsome East African man in a sleek green uniform smiles amiably at her, while an elderly woman in a nightgown unleashes a torrent of Arabic at a porter. But the driver waves at the desk clerk and motions Jay to follow him. "All taken care of, Miss. This way. You're expected." He stops before a closed door at the end of the hall and sets down her bag, presses a key into her hand.

"Here? What do I owe?" fumbling for her wallet.

"All taken care of, Miss. Please. You're expected."

She shoves the bag into the entranceway, shuts the door behind her. She's in a darkened corridor. It's still light outside, but this room, or whatever it is, seems to have every shade drawn tight against the sun. Silence.

"Hello . . . ?"

A shambling, hunched figure looms, lunges at her, making her raise her hands defensively; he encloses her in his arms, this smelly desperate wreck of a man.

"Leland, my god — "

He has her in a fierce hug, pushing her coat off her shoulders, her handbag skittering onto the parquet floor.

"Leland. Hey. What — okay, it's all right — "

He nuzzles her hair and neck hungrily, muttering only, "Thank god thank god thank god," and then he's all over her,

138

hands wandering over her butt and up under her shirt. His breath is sour, he smells of whiskey and sleeplessness and he's got her pinned against the wall now, pushing his hips against her.

"Take it easy. Leland. Holy shit — "

He is rock hard already, lifting her shirt, fumbling with the bra clasp, his breath ragged and guttural. In that moment, she just decides, no doesn't even really decide, just reacts, goes along, reaching behind to undo the hooks for him. This is all the encouragement he needs. Her shirt and underwear are peeled off clumsily, then, impatient, he wrestles her onto the floor. She lies partly on the soft Persian runner, partly on the cool hardwood as he grinds himself into her. He's wild, pumping with a ferocity that feels vicious, but she rides it with him, listening to his gasps of what might be pleasure or just as likely pain. He finishes and falls heavily on top of her, breath coming in sobs, and so still. He's too heavy. She tries to squirm away, but he won't withdraw, just shifts his weight a little. He still has not said her name or anything coherent at all. His hair is lank with grease. She seems to be in a suite of some sort — dimly perceived rooms beyond two, no three doors, all in darkness. When he does eventually speak, his voice is strange — harsh and commanding.

"Do you know what has happened?"

"The driver told me a crisis. But what, Leland?"

"Katie. Gone." He shrinks away inside her and slides out with a juicy sound, shifts to lift himself off her.

She rolls her head back onto the rumpled carpet, closes her eyes. "I am so sorry."

Then she sits up, reaching to gather her scattered clothes, separating his into a pile. She absently strokes his forehead as she rises and pads off in search of the bathroom.

When she emerges from the fortunately well-stocked shower (her own bag remains unopened near the front door), Leland is gone. He has left a note:

The service for my daughter is at St. Mark's, North Findley Street, 11 tomorrow. If you are there, somewhere in the back, perhaps I might bear it.

14.

Church of England high mass, censers, interminable droning about resurrection, the family concealed behind a curtain in an anteroom at the front of the church, and in the crowded pews the cultured world pays its respects. Jay has never seen so many designer iterations of black in one place. All she thought to bring was black levis and a 90s blazer with shoulder pads and torn lining. She speaks to no one, though a scruffy, probably uninvited, mourner who sits behind her at the back mutters, "Not done to give full rites to one that done violence to hersel'. Not done! Shame on 'em!"

Complete silence from the family enclosure. Grief, private. Sorrow and shame hidden from view. She has attended funerals that celebrate a life well lived, and also funerals that gaze bleary-eyed and uncomprehending at a life thrown away. Katie's is certainly the latter.

Leaving the church, a glimpse of the girl's mother? Of Leland's current wife? All the women interchangeably sleek and beautiful. Leland expressionless, wan. Someone has cleaned him up at least, washed his hair, put him in a neat dark suit.

She stands on the church steps and watches the line of limos drive off.

She thinks about Katie's image floating on a screen at the front of the church — a pretty girl, with Leland's narrow face. Some likeness around the eyes too, but lacking his intense, interested directness and curiosity, the gaze already far away. The photo kindly evaded the jutting bones, the hollow cheeks, but that willful detachment from the real world, she knew it, had seen it in her own sister. The crushing logic of the anorexic, an absolute conviction that self-destruction is the only thing that makes sense. Then again, what woman on the threshold of facing all that womanhood requires could argue otherwise?

15.

She's on the couch in the sitting room, marking papers by the light of a single lamp when she hears his key.

"Leland."

It's more than twenty-four hours after the funeral. There's no greeting, just that silent menacing shamble toward her. She can smell it on him, just like the day she arrived. "Don't say it was a lovely service."

"Okay. I won't."

"Don't say anything." And he slouches into the little kitchen, which he has thoughtfully stocked for her: prepackaged Sainsbury dinners for the microwave, fresh milk and fruit and bread. A bottle of wine. Without looking at her, he pours himself a glass of single malt. She steps behind him and reaches into the fridge for the wine. She can feel his eyes on her back, sense the lunge and, though she tries to spin out of his grasp, the room's too small to get past him. The wine bottle drops from her hand but doesn't break, just spins on the floor, striking her ankle; he grabs her by the shoulders, shoving her into the sitting room, toward the couch.

"Leland, you listen to me, dammit — "

He pushes her over the armrest and she falls onto her back, but rolls off before he can pin her. She scrambles to her feet, and stands, poised, with the easy chair between them. She's sober, and he's far from it.

"I will not let you . . . rape me again. Do you hear?"

He stops at this, then swings himself with feline laziness to a sitting position on the couch, regards her with a blandly cruel smile: "Odd word to use. You seemed to like it well enough two days ago."

143

"For god's sake, you used me!"

"'Like' isn't the right word, now that I think about it. You loved it. Or was that somebody else moaning like a hot bitch?" and he springs off the couch at her, but stumbles over the table. "Shit!"

She dodges. "I am not some . . . receptacle."

This stops him. His face twists, an ugly parody: "Oh I *see*."

Jay stands speechless, staring at this unrecognizable creature.

He goes on, raging, "That's how it's done out where you live, is it? What does Oprah recommend? So what we'll do now is hold hands and I'll share my feelings and then we'll both have a nice little cry and feel so much better? Look, Jay, I don't want to *talk* to you. I want to fuck you. Do you have any questions about that? I mean, if you weren't so bloody stupid you'd have figured out all by yourself that there is absolutely not one word to say in this matter that'll make the slightest bit of difference."

She is terrified, reeling. "You're a writer, asshole! Well, aren't you? So find the words. Don't be such a fucking coward." She can hardly hear her own voice for the panic rising in her chest.

He comes at her, slamming his hand on the easy chair, making it spin crazily, then just as suddenly storms back to the kitchen. She hears the glass, the ice cubes, the whiskey gulping from the neck of the bottle into the tumbler.

"I'm — " she begins. Too faint, too shaky. "I'm a writer too, you know. It's terrible beyond words, what's happened, but you have to say it anyway. You know that, don't you?"

"You don't know a damn thing about me."

"You're right."

144

16.

Leland sways slightly as he refills his glass. He can hear her in the next room, importantly shuffling papers, denying him, insisting she knows what he needs. She doesn't. What he needs right now, the only thing that will do, is a piece of ass. And because he loves her more than he's ever loved any woman, he wants it from her. And because, he knows, she loves him more than she ever thought she could love a man, she's going to give him what he needs. Bed posts, yes, at the head of the bed, thank god.

He swallows the whiskey, then pours another and leaves the kitchenette. She glances up at him, her hopeful little face, but he brushes past, into the bedroom, and closes the door behind him. She's not the type for scarves, damn. Well, there's his tie, and . . . what else? His belt? Not flexible enough. Think, think: one more, no, two. His tie and . . . her flannel shirt, that could work and . . . oh, scissors. He bolts back into the living room, noisily opening the desk drawer, and yes, this is a class establishment, the whole array of office supplies thoughtfully provided. She is pretending to mark papers, ignoring him, but he conceals the scissors in his waistband anyway, and returns to the bedroom. He rummages in the dresser drawers: bras, no — ah, the knickers. Feverish now, he fingers through them, selecting a pair of soft cotton, black. He stuffs these into his back pocket, the scissors into the other. The flannel shirt will work just okay, a little awkward, and there's the tie — no wait, save the tie! His trench, her trench! Delighted with himself, he dashes into the hallway. Their two trench coats hang on the rack at the entrance to the suite. The belts are sturdy but soft. Perfect. He secures his navy belt to the left bedpost and her beige one to the right. The scissors — maybe he should leave those on the dresser for now, concealed under something, because what if she grabs them out of his pocket? Yes. Tie in one back pocket, knickers in the other. He's nearly ready. He tries the bedcovers turned down, but then changes his mind and remakes the bed neatly, adjusting the pillows at a comfortable angle.

Leland is excited and happy and utterly absorbed. He takes another sip of his whiskey. Now: getting her into the room. He sips for a while, then goes into the bathroom, comes back out for her empty suitcase. Then stands in the bathroom, grins at himself in the mirror, and throws the suitcase against the toilet. The result is better than he could have hoped. The ceramic lid crashes (but does not break — good luck, that), the towel rack above it rips from the wall and clatters to the tile floor and the thud of the suitcase sounds exactly like a body. He is so pleased he very nearly forgets to shout.

"Uh! oh . . . God. Unnh!"

"Leland? Are you okay?" She's coming. "Le — "

And he's on her, from behind the bathroom door. As she struggles in his arms, it occurs to him that he probably should have thought this through a bit more. He's just strong enough to pin her arms, but she's yelling and he doesn't have a free hand to cover her mouth. She's kicking too. Christ, she's going to fracture his shins. And when he tries to cover her mouth, her free arm flails at his face, pulls his hair. Oh hell, let her scream, it's only another moment. He focuses on just getting her down, that'll help, and encloses her upper body in a tight squeeze, hoisting her feet off the floor and dragging her over to the bed, falling on top of her. It's better like this, he can use

146

his legs to stop the damn kicking. She's still yelling, though; someone might come to the door if he doesn't do something, fast. She's face down, head turned to one side, he's stretched out full length on top of her. He grabs the black underpants, wads them up and, letting her arm go (she can't do much face down anyhow), stuffs her mouth. Her outrage is cartoonish, but he manages to grab her hand back before she can rip the gag out.

He's already tired, and there's still so much to do. So he rests a moment, stretched out full length on her back. The squirming begins to feel quite pleasant; he's getting hard. He presses against her to let her know and makes a grateful, pleased sound in her ear — which makes her lie still immediately.

God, how he loves this woman.

Turning her over is a challenge. He hops up onto hands and knees, flips her and then falls on her again, but her knee connects with his crotch, and she lands a surprisingly good punch to the side of his head, which slows him for a few seconds. But he has a bigger problem. He didn't think to make the loops ready on the end of the belts. Fuck! That's the attraction of handcuffs, one snap and you're done. During the course of these manoeuvres he actually considers trotting down to the nearest naughty shop for supplies, but then dismisses the idea. Too calculated, too tacky. This project must be . . . organic is the best word he can think of at the moment.

So. He'll need two hands for the belts; how, in god's name . . . ? He pins her arms with his knees and when she bucks, he rides her. And she can't kick from this position either, though she tries.

The first arm, the right, is the hardest of course. It takes him a good five minutes of the most wonderful struggle; she pushes the gag out with her tongue, twice, but he gets it back in quickly each time. The nails of her left hand draw blood from his face, and it's so hard to get the bloody knot tied when she won't keep still. He finally has to stretch out full length again, which leaves her left arm free to do its worst and he has to deflect the eye-gouges with his elbow — once, twice, yes, God how she fights — and he pushes her left arm out of his face with a chuckle of the most glorious triumph.

He rests only a few moments before securing the left wrist. Much easier. She seems to be giving up: no more muffled shrieks. Her body goes limp, she has tears in her eyes. He slides down her, holding her still between his thighs. He reaches for her face, gently removing the glasses and setting them on the bedside table, lenses up, of course. Earrings off, watch too. She's nearly pushed the knickers out again — oh no, he forgot the tie but finds it now, turns her head to the side, snugs the striped silk against the freshly wadded black cotton, gently lifting her hair from the back of her head so as not to pull it when he ties the knot.

There. What else? The tears. He brushes them away with a gentle finger, leans close and whispers, "Don't be afraid of me, I promise I won't hurt you."

He has to hop off quickly, just in case she tries another kick. Takes a long slow drink, decides on a refill and a trip to the loo. He can take his time, now.

Leland regards himself in the bathroom mirror as he washes his hands, gives himself a smile. He is startled at how happy he feels at this moment.

Returning to the bedroom, he leaps at her from the side, hops onto her, pinning her between his legs and, humming, removes the scissors from his back pocket. Her whole body lurches in terror, her eyes widen; she tries to squirm away but he places a hand on the centre of her chest, commands, "Lie still." Then, with exaggerated care, lifts her T-shirt six inches off her belly and carefully snips the fabric from the bottom, as if there were an invisible line drawn up the middle of the garment. He gently opens the halves and folds them back. She's wearing a black bra. He's so pleased. He protects her neck with one hand while snipping the cotton jersey from neckline through sleeve — left, then right. Reaches underneath to lift her up from the bed, sliding the mangled T-shirt out from under her and tossing it on the floor. He knows she's watching his every move, but he isn't interested in her eyes, right now. The bra next: straps first, or . . . ? Like a giddy kid, he can't wait; a gentle hand on the solar plexus, a snip between the cups and her breasts are revealed. A snip for each satiny strap. He is very, very hard now. He's going to have to slow down here. Gets up, goes to the dresser, has a deep long drink. Glances over at the bed. She's motionless, acquiescent? Maybe, but probably not quite yet.

Back in position, on her hips. Fly button, zipper, delicious. Massages her hips and arse with strong sure fingers. Tugs gently, stroking the pants right off her, oh hell, might as well take the knickers at the same time, slide them down to her feet.

He contemplates what he has wrought. Leaving one arm on her thighs, he runs a finger between her legs — oh yes, good.

He's ready too. He stands at the foot of the bed and looks into her eyes. He says, softly, "Right, I want to do things to you now. But first you need to say yes."

A small shudder runs through Jay's body. She nods her head.

It's lovely. He can take his time. No violence anymore, that's long gone now, a faint memory. He is trembling with tenderness. He takes time over every inch of her, uses his mouth, tongue, tip of his cock, and his fine white hands. When he gets between her legs, he brings her close, teasing — once, twice, three times. Then he reaches up to remove the tie and knickers. Her eyes are soft, she's moving her hips against him. He knows she won't scream. And besides, he wants to hear the sounds she makes.

And when he brings her, beneath his fingers, she does make some lovely sounds that go right through him like music. She doesn't use any words at all. He leans on one arm looking into her eyes as she rises and trembles in his hand, kisses her deeply, feels the heat and quivering fill his own body.

She's so slippery now that he can't finish there, so he crawls up her prone body, untying the two belts as he rises, and offers himself to her with two words; they sound nice in his ears but are unnecessary, as she takes him into her mouth eagerly. It's over in a moment that seems to last for ever.

He collapses next to her, obliterated, joyous. She lies perfectly still, her eyes soft and deep and quiet. He pulls the covers over them both, encircles her in his arms, whispers, "Sleep now," and like a child she obeys instantly, closing her eyes and nestling against him. He listens as her breathing slows, feels her weight on his arm and chest. Once he knows she's deeply asleep, his tears come, slow and steady and silent. They fall onto her hair, drench the pillow, snake their way down his bare chest.

Katie.

His shoulders shake slightly as he mourns his child, but the weeping is soundless, almost peaceful. He holds a small sleeping woman in his arms; perhaps she's aware of his tears but she does not stir or speak or reach to comfort. She lies perfectly still and trusting in his arms. It's enough.

Part Three

Foothills College, Arts Building, Third Floor

17.

All has gone perfectly according to plan, so far. His silence, his subterfuge, disguise — and he is here, exactly where he wants to be. It's February, the landscape a strange and scary white, the cold so bitter it makes his skull ache. And of course, he's brought all the wrong clothes. The clerk at the hotel reception kindly loaned him a pair of thin woollen gloves, which do little more than keep the wind off his hands; the mind-rattling cold just rips right through.

He finds her classroom: C308. Jay's voice: "Last few minutes, let's just recap. Can you articulate what it was that interested you or pleased you the most about *Jane Eyre*? Yes, Ashley."

"Well, I really like the Rochester character."

"What about the Rochester character?"

"The way he risked everything so he could have Jane? In spite of all the obstacles?"

Jay's exasperation is not audible, and he mentally shakes hands with her for that. She says, "Well, yes. Certainly, the romance plot has its attractions. For one thing, it tends to do what we expect a novel to do. But let's not overlook every-thing else that's going on in this book, all that Bronte has to say about class and gender and society. About what women are permitted to hope for. And how crucial it is that Jane can't have Rochester until the playing field is levelled, first by her sudden wealth, and second by his near-destruction. In short, though she may believe that she can stand at God's feet as any man's equal, in the real world it's an entirely different matter. Until, unless, the man is taken down a peg, until he is blinded, maimed, reduced. Made to atone."

The students shuffle their papers, collect jackets and backpacks with a cacophony of zippers and Velcro.

Leland rests his back against a locker right outside the door. Kensington Suites was nearly four months ago. The first week after she left England, she emailed him several times a day. He shot blanks back, a blank for each four or five messages. Her messages became less frequent, and then trailed off all together. He risks a peek — one student lingers at the desk — and ducks back into the hallway until, apparently satisfied with Jay's answer to her question, the girl makes her way through the door. He watches her pass, then walks in.

She seems embarrassed. Certainly, she wants to get him out of the building as quickly as she can, though a colleague heading into the classroom — a small man, balding but with a tonsure of wispy red hair — recognizes him.

"Oh. My. I didn't know," he stutters. "You know each other? I'm a great admirer of your work."

An introduction has to be made. The man practically drops to his knees, and Leland, annoyed, says only, "Well, thanks so much."

"Are you just here for — "

"A visit. I've been wanting to observe this creature in her natural habitat for some time now," and he gives Jay a squeeze which he feels her resist and surrender to at the same time.

"Well, you've picked a good week: there's a schnook in the forecast," the little man says, gesturing vaguely toward the lowering sun through the tall windows of the corridor.

"How lovely," Leland ventures, but Jay pulls him away, saying, "We'd best get going or we'll miss our train. See you!"

Their trek to the train station (she calls it the C-train, but it's more like a subway that travels above ground) is right out of *Zhivago*, vicious biting winds, ice forming at the tips of his hair, eyes watering; the cold is beyond belief, blistering, how do people live like this? The smell inside the train is overwhelming — sour breath and wet fabric. The windows fog up from the meeting of dry cold and damp human. At each stop, the doors glide open, admitting yet another icy blast, a reminder of what lies outside this fetid shelter. The freeways they pass as the train slides down the rails are concealed in billows of blue exhaust. They speak very little. They are glad to see each other.

"Schnook?" he asks, after a while.

Jay explains "chinook." A native word for a warm wind that comes off the mountains in winter.

Exactly how warm, he wonders, but is content, for now, to wait and see. Perhaps because it has been so long, perhaps because they're both a bit stunned by this sudden reunion, her more so of course, or perhaps because of the long silence between them, she doesn't ask a lot of questions and instead looks intently at him, puts her hands on him: his shoulder, the back of his neck, his knee. She holds his hand on the train, but speaks only when he asks questions.

"What's that?"

"Home Depot. Hardware, stuff for home renovations."

"And that?"

"The Saddledome. Hockey arena."

"And that?"

"Drop-in centre. For the homeless."

If he were talkative, he'd remark that homelessness in this godforsaken wilderness is akin to suicide, but he doesn't, because truly he doesn't much feel like chatting at the moment. He is merely interested in being near Jay. In her presence. With her hand held loosely in his own.

She sizes him up. "Speaking of homeless, you will not survive the twenty minute walk from the station, so . . ." She takes out her mobile and sends a quick message.

Their stop is called and there at the station a venerable Ford van idles, windows frosted over, with a handsome blond boy at the wheel.

Jay's real life seems a kind of dream. The excessively friendly dog, the outwardly indifferent but deeply wary and protective sons. The modest bungalow with paint peeling off the door frames, piles of snow-covered leaves on the lawn.

"The first snow came early this year," Jay says, "right after I got back from London. Oh well, good fertilizer."

Inside, it takes him quite a long time to deal with coat buttons; his fingers are numb, and she offers tea to warm him up. But this is a busy household, and after she has pushed the mug into his hands, she suggests that he make himself at home, have a look around, and busies herself with feeding the dog, checking messages, interviewing the children, preparing the evening meal. It is okay not touching her, because now he's where she lives. And he wanders, with a chipper curiosity, through each of the rooms. Her office — vases containing fragrant dried grasses, stacks of student papers and books. The youngest son's bedroom — the desk a mess of strong-smelling little pots of paint, fierce tiny figures, dwarves it looks like, painted with fervent artistry. Posters of films and rock stars dangling raggedly from the walls, socks and jeans crumpled where they were shed on the floor. Unmade bed.

Ah. Jay's room. This is where he wants to be. Without forethought or shame, he settles in. Squints to study the pictures on the walls, fingers the nightdress and thick velour robe hanging inside the closet door, sifts through the pile of laundry in the plastic basket. Then he opens dresser drawers, runs his hands over balled-up ankle socks in neutral colours, Jockey knickers in cheery shades, swimsuits pushed to the back of the drawers for the season.

The bed. He quietly shuts himself in, hangs his jacket, loosens and removes his tie and his leather belt, and stretches out on what he's certain is the side of the bed she doesn't use.

The life of the household goes on outside the door. He is aware but not aware when she enters the room to softly call him to dinner, then leaving just as quietly when he doesn't respond. She says to her children, "He's fallen asleep. He must be tired after the long flight. Let's just go ahead and have dinner, and then we've got to leave for hockey by 6:45, and what about homework?" The clatter of dishes, the murmur of their conversation. Doors slam, toilets flush, water runs. It's wonderful, this stealthy presence without participation, this semiconscious eavesdropping. She comes in to the room again, rests a hand on his shoulder with a gentleness that thrills him more deeply than any passionate demonstration ever could. She undresses, quietly and quickly; it's pitch dark already. He enjoys the game of guessing, picturing through closed eyes: the woollen blazer, tailored shirt, pleated pants removed, and yes, the change into jeans, cotton T-shirt, no, probably a long-sleeved cotton jersey, turtleneck, yes, and

157

thick socks, against the cold. He loves what he knows already, what he can guess. He wants to know everything.

Loud clatters, thumps, cries of, "Where's my cup?" The sound of a car sliding down the driveway. Then the house falls silent, except for the melancholic huffing of the dog. And voices on the message machine. A girl calls for the eldest son, a high-pitched boy for the younger. An automated message announces that, "You or someone at this number has library materials which are overdue." Australian guy from the video store announces much the same, only live not recorded. Then: "Your son or daughter missed one or more classes today." Automated. Finally, a man calls. "Hi, it's me, guess I missed you guys. I'll try to get to the game, but if I can't get the truck started tonight, I'll just call back later." That one, he hears very clearly. That would be Gray. The sculptor.

An hour passes, maybe two? Leland hears doors slam, zippers open. Something heavy thuds down the stairs to the basement lair of the eldest son. "What a gong show, did you see that hit? The ref shoulda called that!"

The green numbers on the bedside clock glow *9:00*. Morning? No, still night. Water runs, brushes move against teeth, doors open and close, open and close, fridge opens and closes, opens and closes. "Good night." "Night, Mom." The phone rings one more time, around 9:45. "Just arrived out of the blue," Jay says. "I wasn't expecting — I don't *know* . . . I don't know . . . right. Okay. I'll call you tomorrow, right, bye." A gasp of frustration. He hears that.

It's amazing what he hears, as he lies on Jay's bed on this winter night. Dry branches scraping against the window in the wind that rises suddenly. The dog snuffling and scratching.

The startup of the dishwasher, the locking of doors. A young man's voice in the basement, laughing on the phone. And Jay's feet, padding down the hall.

She undresses, again. Sounds like she's putting on the famous tent, which is fine. He wants only to sleep. And again, she doesn't speak, just lays a hand on his shoulder, puts her cheek against his for a moment, then walks around the bed, crawls in her side, curls up with her back to him. It takes a long time for her breathing to deepen. Nearly an hour, he thinks. But after he's waited another hour just to be sure she's asleep, he rises, uses the lav, borrows a neglected-looking toothbrush and returns to her room, stripping down to his shorts and crawling back in, nestling against her carefully. He mustn't wake her.

It's still dark when the alarm rings at 6:10. He doesn't know why he has to feign deep sleep, but that's what he does. He feels her react with shock, at first, at his presence, but she soon orients herself, pushes back against him for a moment, luxuriously. A promise, a welcome.

And their first morning begins.

Footfalls, her voice calling the children's names a first time, then a second, then a testy third. Dishes, the rustling of brown bags, the thud of overloaded backpacks, the knock on the back door. A man's voice: "Hey buddy, set for school? Hang on, I'll give you a lift up the hill. Why don't you go hop in the truck and I'll be out in just a sec — "

Jay's voice, rising, nearly shrill, "Hey, hi. What're you — Jesus, Gray — don't!"

The man's footsteps down the hall, door opening.

159

Leland feels no need to react or move, stays exactly where she left him in the centre of the bed, his bare arm extended over the place where she slept, eyes tightly shut, breathing deep and even. He hears the door close, quietly — and receding footsteps. Jay's voice, "He just showed up, fell fast asleep in my bed, I don't know, I told you, oh for Christ's sake!" Hard footsteps, a door, this one slammed, the roar of an engine. He pictures a menacing billow of blue smoke.

The house falls silent. So silent that he really does fall back to sleep, for a while. Until he senses her in the room again, at the foot of bed. Now. Now it can all start. And he lifts his head from the pillow. "Good morning."

"Hi. You slept a long time."

"Yes. I did. Come here."

He opens his arms and watches as, without hesitation or self-consciousness, she raises the flannelette tent over her head, lets it drop to the floor and moves swiftly toward him.

Afterwards, nestled together, he says, "So your other man was here this morning."

"Yes."

"What did he say?"

She pulls away and turns to look at him. "What do you think he said, Leland? He was here, he was pissed. Is that what you want?"

"Jay, the reason I am here is to try to answer that very question." He pulls her back into his arms and, breathing into her hair, says, "You know, I haven't been with a woman since the last time I was with you."

She thinks about this for a moment. "I can only imagine how rough it's been."

"You seem to have had no difficulty keeping yourself occupied."

"Hey, you dumped *me*, remember? What the hell was I supposed to do?"

A long silence, then.

It's nearly noon when she rouses him, pulls back the bedcovers. Outside, water runs. The pale white sun of yesterday replaced by clear blue sky and golden light. "Ah," Leland mutters. "The foehn."

"The what?"

"Your chinook. This happens in Austria too. This type of winter wind. They call it the foehn."

The temperature outside has gone from minus thirty to plus five, and it rises steadily through the busy afternoon. Because Leland has, apparently, arrived just in time for Teacher's Convention, in which every schoolteacher in the province has to convene, while every student in the province gets a four-day weekend. This bizarre annual rite, he discovers, gives rise to a range of preparations. They drive to the mall, pass a car bearing a bumper sticker that reads *Jesus loves you. Everyone else thinks you're an asshole.* Inside the supermarket, while Jay tosses packets, cartons and plastic jugs into the shopping cart, a chirpy woman on the loudspeaker advises shoppers to consider all the good things one's nose does, and to reward said nose for its hard work by purchasing Safeway Aloe Vera facial tissues. Back at home, she leads him into the basement, rummages in storage closets and cardboard boxes to assemble for him an outfit of winter clothing that makes him look and feel like a teddy bear made of polymer microfibres. "But it's warm outside now, the chinook!" he protests, feeling bulky, sweaty and foolish, particularly about the watchcap, which she insists on calling a "tewk".

"Chinooks sometimes last a week, sometimes just a few hours," she asserts, and zips the Board Doktor jacket up to his chin. The next step, and time is running short now, is loading the car, because they need to "swoop" (Jay's word) by the two schools in less than an hour. They must be on the highway the moment the boys get out of school, so as to reach their destination before nightfall, which comes early at this time of year.

"Why before dark?" Leland asks.

"One, because I have lousy night vision, and two, ninety percent of the roadkill happens at night." Seeing his puzzled and fearful expression, she adds, "I mean deer and elk and such."

"Can you elaborate on 'such'?"

"Here, hold these." And the two of them scramble to load the van with supplies: grocery bags and coolers, cases of pop and beer, the dog, snowboards and boots, skiis, ski poles and boots, skates and hockey sticks, a couple of snow shovels, a toboggan, a bag of books, newspapers, CDs, and old movies on videocassette. And cold weather wear for the four of them: jackets, ski pants, boots, mitts, neck warmers, hats, scarves, goggles, thick socks, and longjohns. This collection of clothing strikes Leland as particularly odd, given that now, at nearly 3:00 PM, the mercury has risen to seventeen degrees, and people pass on the street in shirtsleeves. At the schools, some of the students wear sneakers and shorts. The music of coursing water from melting snow fills the city as they drive west, toward the mountains.

At the cabin, Jay says, "Whether by design or accident, I have managed to be a pretty good role model for Ben and Danny all these years. My private life is private, and as far as they're concerned, men and women don't sleep together if they're not married, or at least committed. So I'm going to ask you to sleep in the guest room. The boys can share the bunk room like always, and I'll be in the master."

He grudgingly goes along with this the first night, though he finds the temptation of a brief nocturnal visit almost irresistible. He makes an opportunity, the next day, to talk to each of her sons. With the youngest, his pitch is very straight-forward: "Look, mate, I'm dead keen on your mom, you know that, right? Now she seems to think you'd be bent out of shape if I were to share a bed with her, but I don't think she's right about that, do you?"

The boy replies, "Aw, no big deal. Dad's girlfriends stay over all the time."

With the elder, Leland knows, the matter must be broached rather more cautiously. The two of them have been sent round the side of the house for firewood, and as the boy stacks logs into his outstretched arms, he says, "Man to man, Ben. You know what it's like to want to be with a woman, right? Well, I feel that way about your mother. She figures you'll object if we sleep in the same room, but I think she doesn't give you guys nearly enough credit. What do you think?"

The boy says nothing, keeps piling the logs 'til they're nearly to his chin — *Christ, oh Christ he wants to kill me, oh*

Christ my back — but then Ben stops, grabs the top four or five logs off Leland's quivering arms and coldly smiles, "Actually, Leland, I'm not cool with that. Mom's with Gray," and heads back toward the house.

On their second full day, Jay gets up early, drives the kids to the ski hill, and then returns to the cabin, where Leland waits before the fire, which he has learned to construct, feed, and maintain. And it's then, over cups of tea, that he tells her of the quiet mutual agreement of separation he has obtained from Christa. (He does not mention the cost of this agreement, which was enormous, and she doesn't ask.) It's then also that he speaks of Meg. His mistress. An abbreviated tale of their four raucous years, ending with the breakup a few months ago. It disturbs him a bit that Jay hears him out so calmly, appears so unsurprised. He says nothing about her man, though. He has decided to give her time.

Toward the end of that long, drowsy day, he surprises himself by saying, "My guess is that we're stuck into this now. We pretty well have to go on from here, I think." Until that moment, he hasn't been exactly sure what he came here to accomplish. But now in this beautiful strange peaceful place, the way forward seems clear.

Next day there's a hockey game on the freshly scraped ice of the lake, a cleared section about thirty metres square. Jay and her kids generously allow him to eschew skates and put him in goal with his feet encased in bloody big clodding snowboots. Then the rest of them fire tennis balls at him with hockey sticks, Ben taking a few particularly hard shots at his crotch. But even he eases up after a while, and Leland just stands watching Jay and her boys circling and swooping on their skates like sailboats, like shorebirds, chanting, "Get it through the *five*-hole, get it through the *five*-hole!" At one pause in play, he and Jay watch the dog take off after a herd of elk, laughing themselves silly at her foolish doggy heart, as if she has the ghost of a chance to outrun, not to mention bring down, a single one.

He holds Jay in the dark before bed, then goes out on the deck. The nights are so cold and clear and black and utterly, utterly silent that he knows himself to be fully alone in the world. The sky so purely dark that it makes no difference whether he opens his eyes or not. Behind his closed eyelids, a little girl moves in dappled sunlight, counting off to ten, chubby hands covering her eyes. Katie finds him here, a lonely figure surrounded by dark mountains, under a black sky.

On their return to Calgary, he's introduced to Jay's mother in her rest home. Mara, a sweet, still pretty woman of seventy-five, stroke victim, welcomes him warmly — "I like your accent" — with a flirtatious gleam in her bright blue eyes. "Where's Gray?"

As always with women and their mothers, it occurs to him that this old woman is what Jay will become.

"Gray's not here," Jay says. "This is my friend from England. Leland."

Mara brightens. "I've been to England. We always ate in the pubs. The food was much cheaper, and really very good."

Leland says, "Pub food has always been a favourite of mine."

"In Wales," Mara goes on, "we stopped to ask directions, and this little old man stood there and talked and pointed, and well we nodded and smiled and said thank you very much but you know, it's a funny thing, he was speaking English but not one of us understood a single word."

"Yes." Leland smiles. "The Welsh accent can be very thick."

Mara smiles back. He is passing the test. "I'm glad Jay has a friend from England. I always ordered the ploughman's lunch. Where's Gray?"

In the car on the way back to Jay's place, the radio plays one 80s tune after another on the classic rock station. He proves that he knows every word to every tune including Bon Jovi's "Livin' on a Prayer," by singing as loud as he can.

"Oh do shut up," is Jay's response.

"I can't help it," he says. "I was single through the mid 80s, out clubbing a lot. The songs just stuck."

"Well, while you were out clubbing, I was stuck at home changing diapers. The only adult voices I heard all day were Peter Gzowski and Erika Ritter."

"Who are they?"

Now, Leland is going home. To all that is familiar, the good and the bad of it. Not single, not married, somewhat betrothed, perhaps. Work to do. Bereaved father. Someone who must write, despite everything, because it's all he really knows how to do. And on his flight back to London as he tries to decide which moment goes deepest — sitting quietly with Jay before the fire, or the hilarity of the hockey match, or the deep silence of the mountain night — she shows up again. Katie. And as always, she's speaking the last words she said to him: "You selfish prick! First you cheat on my mother, and now you cheat on the woman you left us for! What is *wrong*

166

with you?" Thrusting at him that small newspaper clipping from a tabloid: *And what literary lion was observed recently slinking out of the hotel room of a visiting Canadian writer quite early one morning?*

He remembers mornings. Katie was a lark, like him, a morning star. Early riser. My girl. There she is, oh about four years old, toddling into the kitchen, table set for the two of us, and she loved corn flakes, hungry, every morning, hungry, and she pours her cereal into her bunny bowl, and her little hand comes up, and pats the cereal down flat in the bowl, in the morning light her little hand, patting the cereal flat before pouring on the milk, and takes her first bite — yes, and then this little groan of pleasure, of satisfaction.

Part Four

A Dinner Party, London, Early May

18.

On a street corner in Knightsbridge, a mild evening in spring, a tall man and a smallish woman contend. Step, drag, stall.

"You're making us late — "

"Just give me another minute, that's all — "

"Jay!" A sharp tug. "You're with me, remember?" And he drags her the last half block, up gleaming stairs of scrubbed white stone with polished wrought-iron hand rail to a door painted a hectic red, which is abruptly opened by an overexcited Irishwoman in her sixties.

"At last! Leland. And ah — here's the wee lass. I'm Lucille, dear. Come in, we've all — Howard! They've arrived, everyone! They're here at last."

And Jay is tugged into a blur of shockingly expensive good taste, famous erudition, and loud, loud voices, a Babel of them that makes her think of barking dogs. Foxhounds. Terror and shyness render her utterly stupid, completely mute beyond "hello" and "pleased to meet you." She is careful to say, "Meet you," and not "Meetcha," but beyond that —

Leland does his share, though, and a good chunk of hers. She has now been generally introduced as "the bride-to-be" and then to individuals as, "My Canadian wench, guess I've no choice but to make an honest woman of her." She clings to his arm, but in time, as he must, he moves away and she's trapped in a gaggle of toothy inquisitive women, varied by the occasional silky gay man in exquisite clothes — one wears a blue pinstripe shirt so fine she has to grab her own hand to keep it from stroking the fabric. She wonders, what ever happened to that famous British reserve that Austen and Drabble assert, and she has always accepted as cultural fact?

"You must tell us how you met, was it over that little book of yours?" asks one.

"Oh my, yes," says another, "*Richdale* was such fun."

Five years of my blood and bones adds up to fun? you snotty bitch! "Thank you."

"I must say I don't think I've ever seen Leland so — and I have known this man well for thirty-odd years — well, he's absolutely . . . radiant."

Perhaps he's pregnant. Shy smile, equally radiant, she hopes.

"Yes, you must reveal your secret — "

Frequent blow jobs. "Well. I like him, he likes me, I guess."

"Of course you'll live in London, I couldn't imagine Leland — well all that snow for one thing, and oh, theatre, galleries, what possibly would he do?"

Like when that literary star from Toronto took a job at the University of Calgary and the Globe *practically wrote the guy a eulogy, so bloody insulting.* "Actually, there's a very vibrant arts community in my hometown, excellent theatre, great music."

"Where exactly is . . . Alberta, is that the name?"

In Texas, just across the river from Alaska. "One province east of Vancouver."

Jay can hear Leland across the room, performing: "And she says, 'No shit, Sherlock'! But the best was — I'll never forget it, I fell in love with her that moment — I'd said something singularly witless and manlike, and she stepped in front of me, said, 'Look, let me explain something to you.' She taps the side of my head and says, 'This for thinkin',' and then she pokes me, uh, below the belt and says, 'and this is for fuckin'. You got that?'"

170

His listeners reward him with delighted laughter. He's got her accent just right: dropped 'g's, and "fer" instead of "for." A woman has materialized beside her — perfume and cigarettes and gin. "You're not what I expected at all."

She's a wiry little woman, late forties perhaps, masterfully and expensively preserved. A sparkling dress that probably cost more than Jay makes in six months. The woman's hair has a metallic sheen. Her lipstick is an arch, sadistic maroon.

Jays sips her drink. "I don't believe we've met. I'm — "

"Oh, I know who you are."

"And your name is?"

"Don't let him get kinky on you, take my advice. He goes too far. In some ways, I think him a deeply disturbed individual."

"Hmm. I've been wondering exactly what it is we have in common."

The woman makes sudden but fleeting eye contact, then looks away. She mutters, "You should be proud of yourself. You've succeeded where half the women in London have failed."

"Yourself included?"

"I could tell you stories."

"I'd rather you didn't. Excuse me." *Bathroom, bathroom, Jesus Christ, fresh air, goddammit where the hell is —*

"You're looking a bit peaky, dear." Their hostess, Lucille. Recognizably human. "Come here, come along. This way."

It's a lovely little room, a study. Dark bookshelves, two soft plushy chairs arranged before a gas fire turned low. Lucille gives her a gentle shove into one of the chairs, and sinks into the other. "There. Take a moment. I don't know what he could

171

be thinking, trotting you out like this, like a prize spaniel. Men can be so dense."

"Thanks. I was feeling, um, a little overwhelmed."

"I don't blame you. Well, I've pulled you out of the fray for a short while at least. Shall I go and find Leland? Tell him you're here?"

"No. No, thanks. I'd like to just — "

"Of course. Jay, you're just right for him. I feel it, I really do. I've known this man for many years. He's difficult, he's complicated. You understand, though, how shall I say this? Trust him, but trust yourself more."

"How do I do that?"

"Keep something back, always. Just a little piece, but something. You'd be wise."

"All right."

"I'm needed in the kitchen. I'll send someone down when we're ready. I've got you a very good safe place at the table."

"Lucille, you've been very kind."

Unlike plump Lucille and her tweedy husband, the table is sleek, stylish, minimalist. The food is artfully presented, the edible indistinguishable from the garnish. Silence is her best defence, she decides. So she sits and listens to and smiles at a spirited debate on a recent *TLS* commentary on narrativity, episodic or diachronic. Thence to the question raised recently in the *Spectator* about whether Dickens was our greatest letter writer, or Johnson. Lucille has placed Leland next to Jay, of course, and her own harmless husband on the other side; the sleek nasty woman has disappeared altogether (perhaps she was only invited for cocktails?) But across and a couple of places down, there he is. The curmudgeon with father issues. He settles for sneering looks 'til the main course arrives, then —

"So, Jay, tell me — it is Jay, isn't it?"

"That's right."

"As in just a letter, a cipher rather than a name."

"No. As in J-A-Y. As in blue jay. The bird. No relation to the baseball team though."

"How interesting. So tell me, Jay, it's been nagging at me, at so many of us over here for some time, where the fuck, exactly, is Skookumchuck? And, how in god's name did you ever persuade an urbane fellow such as Mackenzie to ever accompany you to such a place, much less propose marriage there?"

"Second question is none of your business, but Skookumchuck," Jay begins, aware of the general conversation dying away all down the table, one mouth at a time, "is a very beautiful peaceful place that, for my money, anyone fool enough to refuse the chance to spend time there is . . . well, not worth bothering with. As to the first question, it's at the Western edge of the Rockies. The Rocky Mountains. On Highway 95, or rather five miles down a logging road off 95, about twenty clicks south of Canal Flats. If you climb Saddleback, you can see all the way to Banff."

"All the way to Banff? From Saddle — "

"Back."

Leland is aware now, please god don't let him, but he chimes in, damn him — "Canal Flats being about forty clicks south of Dry Gulch. And of course we always stop at the Husky at Deadman's Flats for coffee when we head out there."

The curmudgeon's eyes sparkle. "South of Caaannaayl Flaaats, you say? How interesting."

Jay expels every millimeter of air from her lungs, then fills them deeply again. "Pardon me, but you're pronouncing it wrong. That's a Deep South cracker accent you're using. You know, the string 'em up, drag 'em behind the pickup for fun on a Saturday night variety. The long 'A' is just dead wrong."

"Clearly I require some instruction."

"Think of the map of North America. Deep south just above that little dick that's Florida. Then draw a line diagonally northwest 'til you hit some bumps — "

"So how does one say Canal Flats then?"

"Western Canadians use a very short dry 'a'. Yours is too toff, too plummy, too 'playing fields of Eton.' Say it like that at the truck stop and I guarantee, at best, that the waitress will spit in your tea."

"A daunting thought. Perhaps, however — "

"So go ahead, try it. Short clipped 'a'. Canal Flats."

Hateful look, silence.

"Or try this, what do you call your mother's sister?"

"Windy old bitch."

"Perhaps, but how do name her?"

"She's my awnt, of course."

"Right. Say 'ant' now, like the insect. That's what you're after."

The man's mouth twitches; Lucille trills, "What can I pass, now? Who needs more salad?"

"Just trying to be helpful," Jay says to him. "I'd feel awful if you got the crap beaten out of you at the Wasa Pub at Leland's stag."

174

Conversation at Lucille's table is at a standstill. Howard tries a faint laugh, the woman across from Jay sneezes loudly, But Jay owes her hosts . . . something, so she attempts a mitigation: "I'll never forget the time my friend Bernadette went to the Skookumchuck general store; she's French, Paris-born. And when she asked for a 'bus ticket' the clerk somehow heard 'birthday cake' and a huge argument ensued, with this clerk insisting no, we don't sell birthday cake here and my friend, with that high dudgeon the French have perfected, points to the sign on the wall advertising Greyhound and says, 'So what, may I ask, is ZAT?'"

Polite chuckles, then rescue, as Leland gamely wades in, "And of course there was the time I stood at the meat counter at the local supermarket, insisting that all I needed was a pack of mince, and the blood-spattered gent took me by the arm and stood me up in front of the candy rack, shoved a packet of Scotch mints into my hand!"

Jay stuffs something that might be food into her mouth and keeps her eyes down. She counts to sixty, then makes herself count to sixty again, 'til the table noise has risen close to its previous level, and she can mutter, "Excuse me," and push back her chair.

She keeps herself together until she gets the bathroom door closed behind her. Then she falls apart, shaking, feeling like she's about to wet her pants, every internal organ wanting to liquefy. Braces her arms on the vanity, head down, afraid to meet her own gaze, and it must be several minutes though it feels like mere seconds when she hears Leland outside the door. She ignores the first soft raps, ignores his pleading voice. But he is insistent: "Jay. You must let me in."

She opens the door and he wraps his arms around her. "You were magnificent."

"I'm scared shitless."

"I'm proud of you."

"He'll go after me again, I just know it. I can't go back out there, I just can't."

"You have to. I'll be right there."

"Yeah, right."

"What's that supposed to mean?"

The words come out before she has even noticed they're in her head. "Leland, sometimes I wish you could find me a little less amusing, you know. In public, I mean."

"Oh, for Christ's sake — "

"I'm not an experience you're having. Okay?"

"Oh my dear — "

"Swear to God, Leland, if you call me 'little one' right now, I will plunge a knife through your heart."

"The place you're from is not you, all right?"

"Well, it isn't. But it is. The same goes for you, you know."

"Perhaps. I think Henry James had it right — in *Washington Square* — you know, when what's his name, Maurice, says, *You would not want me without my attributes.* I know I wouldn't want you without your attributes. And you probably wouldn't want me without mine. Isn't that right? Come back to the table. Soon."

She successfully avoids the curmudgeon for the remainder of the evening; in fact, she's surprised and gratified at how generously the other guests, to a man and woman, join forces to shield her (or possibly her hosts, or Leland, or more likely the simple idea of social decorum) by engaging the two

176

antagonists in separate animated conversations until the meal ends, and the guests begin to disperse. Only on one brief occasion does she pass close to him on her way to the kitchen with a load of dessert plates, and overhears, "Amazing really. No little hat with fishing lures ranged along the band. I'm so disappointed."

Part Five

What Happens Next

19.

From: jmcnair@telus.net
To: lcMackenzie@hotmail.com
Date: May 27 9:10 AM
Subject: thanks for
The memories. My first London dinner party. Remind me to never accept a similar invitation again. Kidding aside, though, it just occurred to me — Jesus, you must think me shockingly naïve — but it just now occurs to me that the reason I got invited to read in London this time last year was . . . because of you. I mean, you did something, spoke to someone. Didn't you?

From: lcMackenzie@hotmail.com
To: jmcnair@telus.net
Date: May 28 11:05 PM
Subject: the facts, jack
It would be a fine thing if literary publishing were a merit-ocracy, but it is not. Why, just last night, for political reasons, I was forced to sit through an interminable reading by a young poet in whom the ratio of ambition to actual talent is greater than three to one. Why was she standing there when others, so much better, cleaner, pleasure-giving, toil away unknown but to those who love them?

Jay, if I can do some small thing, I do it gladly. I'd prefer not to discuss what, if anything, I may or may not do to be helpful to you. Can we set that aside, please? If I offer to dry the dishes, or carry in the groceries, or lift something too heavy for you, there's no need for gratitude. And there's no need on this other, too. I help if I can, if I may.

From: jmcnair@telus.net
To: lcMackenzie@hotmail.com
Date: May 29 9:45 AM
Subject: Yes, but

Oh dear. I can't make up my mind. Is it about just helping out, just lifting and fetching and carrying? I keep thinking about what Berger says in *Ways of Seeing*. You know, how the image of a man speaks of what he can do to you or for you, whereas the image of a woman speaks of what can be done to her and for her. I can't . . . sort this through, Leland. If you didn't offer to carry in the groceries, I'd think you a total asshole. If you do speak my name or whisper *Richdale* in the ear of someone who might do the book some good . . . oh I don't know. This confuses the hell out of me.

How's the new flat? How's the squash game? Are you looking forward to Hay on Wye?

From: lcMackenzie@hotmail.com
To: jmcnair@telus.net
Date: June 15 3:10 PM
Subject: Wye note

Berger also very rightly points out that art is a commodity, in addition to . . . what ever else it might aspire to be, and that those who become sentimental about that, who take the moral high ground, merely refuse to see what is really there.

The Hay Festival a delight as always. Lovely setting, convivial company, wonderful food and drink. Always a pleasure to watch your dinner party nemesis drink too much and make a fool of himself over some young thing. My stints on stage were mercifully brief and no-one threw things at me. Remember that line in *The Smoking Diaries* where Simon is at Toronto and he pulls out the measuring stick for who has the longest line for book-signings? Doesn't he say that "a quarter of a dozen" people lined up at his table, while the line for David Lodge seemed, to poor old Simon at least, to go out into the lobby, down the motorway and all the way to the airport?

Well, my dear, you will be pleased to hear that mine was longer than the curmudgeon's. Much, much longer. But I expect you knew that already. Instinctively, I mean. Not actually. Not practically, I hope. Oh my.

From: jmcnair@telus.net
To: lcMackenzie@hotmail.com
Date: June 16 9:20AM
Subject: size matters
Size doesn't matter.

Yes it does and I am . . . um, fully satisfied with facilities on offer . . . oh dear.

But Leland, despite the long separations, can we please resist cyber sex and phone sex? I mean, I don't mind the occasional phrase like "your nipple stiffening against my hand" for example — I remember that line, it has a lovely resonance, and I do recall it, and the sensation it describes, often and with pleasure. But let's be cautious about this, okay? To be doing the fuck-me-baby thing from a distance is just . . . crass.

_____

From: lcMackenzie@hotmail.com
To: jmcnair@telus.net
Date: June 18 12:10 AM
Subject: decorum
I couldn't agree more.
Love,
L
PS Fuck me baby

Part Six

Summer, then Winter

20.

British Airways Flt 034, to London, August

Leland is remembering the play of light on Jay's shoulders, her sleek head breaking green water. And in the speedboat, how the kids laughed at his panic — "Stop! she's falling, Christ!" "No, man she's just dropping the ski, she's going slalom" — and there she was, skimming the lake, grinning, raising rainbowed arcs of water at the outer curve of each graceful turn.

He did not know that water could be so cold. After immersion in such water, nothing looks so pitiful as a man's private parts and nothing tastes so good as a hot cup of tea. She does not know who Alan Bennett is. She's never heard of *Beyond the Fringe*. He is keeping a list for her: an imperial education, she calls it, and claims she does not need to know such things, she will know them if her curiosity is adequately piqued. She seems oddly content with her . . . context, her limited view. This puzzles him, frankly. How could she not want to know what any literate person, but most particularly any writer, must know? She has such a good mind, a lively soul, how could she be content —

Labour Day, Skookumchuck

A hot and still and clear day, belying summer's end. Jay sits on the deck with her oldest friend. The boys have gone off to the cliffs in the runabout, so the two women risk an after-dinner joint, just prior to Leland's taped broadcast on CBC, his eulogy for the Salinger biographer, Ian Hamilton. Which the two of them listen to on the radio balanced on the planks.

Jay wishes she hadn't smoked that joint. She wishes Leland hadn't referred to Salinger as "Jerry" quite so often. She wishes his voice didn't override the softer voice of the other commentator, a man who obviously knew Hamilton better and cared about him more. She wishes that Leland's comments, in his tribute, this eulogy, would begin less often with the words *when I was* and *I felt then that* — When the interview ends, she finds nothing to say. Her friend takes a breath, looks across at the lake. "Well. He's very well read, isn't he? That man of yours."

It's the joint, it must be. She really really wishes she hadn't smoked that joint.

From: jmcnair@telus.net
To: lcMackenzie@hotmail.com
Date: September 15 9:20 AM
Subject: re: Mr. Mackenzie regrets
Hey guy: Good to talk to you last night. Seriously, Leland, no sweat about having to cancel your Thanksgiving visit. Yes, I'm sure you were just dying to sample my legendarily disastrous attempt at a turkey dinner. But I remember what it's like to be on the home stretch with a manuscript. Keep your head down. Go for it, dude.

Love,

J

_____

From: lcMackenzie@hotmail.com
To: jmcnair@telus.net
Date: October 10 11:55 PM
Subject: what I meant was
Well, no of course I don't have a fucking clue what kind
of Scotch Mordecai Richler drank, and as to the identity of
the lampooned party in the Atwood story you mentioned I
am entirely innocent. Your reaction surprised me, frankly. I
was merely recommending a book, Jay. Written by a friend of
mine. One that I like very much. The book and the friend, I
mean.

Lucille got all fluttery at tea Monday over "setting the date,"
by the way. I know you want to keep an eye on your mum,
though . . . oh hell. I'll give you a call this weekend, okay?

With fondest love from your colonial oppressor

L

_____

From: jmcnair@telus.net
To: lcMackenzie@hotmail.com
Date: October 24 8:10 AM
Subject: the empire whines back
Next time she corners you like that, just tell Lucille you've
decided not to marry me because you realized that I'd make a
shitty wife. Tell her that you know this because I said to you,
recently, "I'd make a really shitty wife." And actually, I did
make a fairly shitty wife, you know. Well, I was good at some
parts of the job. Fidelity I had no trouble with. Loyalty either.
But "adoring" came hard, and "long-suffering" I didn't do well
AT ALL.

I really do think that all this romance stuff gets it backwards: that it's men who want to be adored. Women just want to be taken seriously.

Let's just have an affair that lasts forever. What do you say?

Love,

J

From: lcMackenzie@hotmail.com

To: jmcnair@telus.net

Date: October 30 11:50 PM

Subject: adorable

It really is absolutely adorable, the way you can use the word "shitty" so many times in a single paragraph. Did you see my piece on Hamilton in the *Guardian* mag? I've gotten good feedback on it here. Sorry to hear of Mara's turn for the worse, Jay. What do the doctors say? Do you want me to come?

Love,

L

21.

Agape Manor Hospice Calgary, November

The impossibly shiny corridors. The worn plaid chairs in the family lounge. She's sitting with a rolled-up copy of a magazine in her hand, willing her breathing to slow, willing her heart to quiet, willing that thick nausea back down down down —

Gray touches her shoulder, "You'll be all right, Jay, you're doing great."

Not caring, ready to plead grief's derangement, she merely smiles through tears. Then she rises, twists the *Guardian* magazine containing that supposed tribute that's really just a long advertisement for Leland's own brilliance, and tosses it in the garbage can (*not rubbish bin!*) before returning to Mara's bedside.

London, November

Being so caught up with the pre-Christmas publishing rush, the frenzied round of readings, events, launches, Leland nearly misses Jay's email, her sad but not unexpected news. She states very clearly that she does not want him to attend the funeral. She reminds him that he has already said his goodbyes when he visited Mara in the rest home last summer, and even then her mom didn't know him, didn't remember, kept calling him by the wrong name. "My biggest regret, of course," Jay writes, "is that I dismissed her even more readily than she dismissed herself. And my greatest fear is that I was so intent on becoming exactly NOT-HER that, in so many ways, I became her."

Leland tries several drafts of his response: "Whatever her failings, she gave me the most wonderful gift, she gave me you — " No, too sappy. "Whatever her indecisions, her refusal to act or choose, she gave rise to you, she opened the door for you." None of it works, though, and he books a flight.

22.

It's late, after eleven, on a blustery November night. Jay is wrapping up the leftover sandwiches, when Ben yawns through the kitchen. "How come Leland was at the funeral but not at the reception? It's weird that he didn't come."

"What?"

"Leland. Reception. Didn't come."

"Leland wasn't at the funeral."

"Yes he was, way in the back. I talked to him when I went out to use the can."

"But I wrote him about Gramma and told him not to come! Jesus, Ben, why didn't you tell me?"

Her boy smiles wearily. "Jesus, Mom! Because I thought you knew! I'll finish this up if you like." And he drapes his arm over her shoulder, kisses the top of her head.

Leland is not hard to find. Same hotel as last winter, the International. The desk clerk gets a little snotty with her, justifiably so, as it's very late and she looks and acts like a crazy woman. But the guest picks up on the first ring and gives the okay.

He's still up, still dressed, his laptop on. He's had a bit to drink, but not too much. "I watched you. With your boys, with your man. And it surprised me really, the sense of relief. She's okay, I thought, she's fine."

"Look, Leland, it's the death, that's what it is, I needed — "

Leland raises a hand, backs her off. "Jay, it occurs to me that really, all that can be obtained — no, not obtained, but received — from this, this gift, because that's what it is, what it was — well, we have it all already. We've used it up."

190

"Leland. No."

"To continue would be foolish. We can't continue. That's clear."

"Look, I called Gray a week before Mom died. A lot of old people die this time of year, around the first frost, first snowfall. As if they just can't be bothered to go through another winter. I hadn't talked to him for six months, but the rest home called and I went to see her and, obviously it wouldn't be long now and, I don't know, I just felt . . . " And at that moment, the will to fight just leaves her. She meets Leland's steady gaze. "He's someone I know, someone who knows me." A deep breath. "Who likes me the way I am."

Leland drains his glass, sets it down on the table. Then turns to her, says "Well, Jay. There you go."

She lifts her coat from the chair as if to leave, but then turns back.

"But don't kid yourself that this is about Gray, because you know as well as I do that it isn't. I thought you had something I needed, but it turns out that the space you take up in my life is just too big. I can't spare it." She takes a step toward him. "And, admit it, ever since Katie, you've been telling yourself some story of redemption, but really . . . Leland?"

They look at each other, a long deep look in which is distilled at last a moment of the most perfect and unblemished communion: the truth of what she wanted from him, and he from her, laid bare. Her foolish hope of putting on his knowledge with his power, his impossible desire to atone —

"But really," he agrees at last, "I would have lost Katie anyway, whether I'd met you or not."

"Yes."

Oddly, what's in his eyes at that moment is the glimmer of a self-deprecating smile.

And in the air between them as they say goodbye there's a weird ineffable grace, something oddly like forgiveness.

23.

From: lcMackenzie@hotmail.com
To: jmcnair@telus.net
Date: January 11 3:00 PM
Subject: Final email, final draft:

I think now that you and I came together not for joy but for blood and tearing. (Yes I know that's Elizabeth Smart, and yes I know she's Canadian. And Barker was an asshole Brit, I know that too.)

Thank you, for blood and tearing.

(Though unlike Barker, I did in fact leave my wife.)

Please don't reply, Jay. Shoot me a blank so I know you've received this, but please don't reply.

From: jmcnair@telus.net
To: lcMackenzie@hotmail.com
Date: January 11 11:55 PM
Subject: no subject

Times Literary Supplement: July, two years later

The newest Mackenzie is a departure; this voice is unlike any we've heard from this acclaimed author of serious literary yet widely read fictions about contemporary life. In *The Woman at the Top of the Stairs*, Mackenzie crosses cultures and epochs to craft a story of love, romantic and paternal, that is at once dreamlike and vividly sensual. He abandons his customary decorum and reserve at every artistic level, weaving a story that might move even the most jaded reader to startled laughter and quiet tears.

Globe and Mail Book Review: one year after that

Jay McNair has built her reputation by sheer cheek; she deals in a kind of self-disparaging irony that has attracted a narrow if devoted following among the perimenopausal set. But with *Definition*, McNair has matured. She has, dare I say it, learned to take herself and her art seriously, and the result is smashing.

A HAPPY PRISONER REVISITED

At least Royland knew he had been a true diviner.
There were the wells, proof positive. Water. Real wet
water. There to be felt and tasted. Morag's magic
tricks were of a different order. She would never
know whether they actually worked or not, or to
what extent. That wasn't given to her to know. In a
sense, it did not matter. The necessary doing of the
thing — that mattered.

The Diviners, Margaret Laurence

Everything that's grim about November gathers around me as I trundle to the car after the last class of the day. Louring skies, a menacing chill in the air, all colour leached from the world, everything dull grey and brown, not yet brightened by snow. The Canlit survey class on Atwood's early stories went pretty well. Okay, so "Rape Fantasies" was probably a bit dated for them, in their world of instant porn. But I think they got a kick out of the title story, "Dancing Girls."

But there was that strange moment in the discussion of "Rape Fantasies." Determined to get a rise out of them, I said: "This narrator seems to think that she is simply being an honest woman. Is she self-deceived?"

Not one student made eye contact — which usually means they haven't read the story. But not always.

Then I sensed movement and muttering from the back of the room. "Yes? Did you have a comment? Is it Renee?" I still haven't got all the names straight. The girl is pale, shy. Red-faced.

"Umm," she mutters — and I don't want to push.

But then the chatty young man in the next desk says, "Well, it's sort of a 'lie back and enjoy it' kind of thing, isn't it, Professor Mair? Pretty old school?"

"No," Renee says, with surprising force. "I just think that the only people who enjoy rape fantasies must be people who've never been raped."

A beat.

I say, "You know, that's a potent suggestion. Yes. To take the position that the narrator of 'Rape Fantasies' takes is to claim a kind of privileged ignorance, isn't it?"

An icy wind wraps itself around my ungloved hands as I dump books and files into the back seat and start the car. I wonder, now that I've gotten to the end of *Final Draft*, to the end of Leland and Jay, whether things will settle down. Maybe the real world will begin to seem adequate again, maybe even interesting, maybe even promising. Maybe even real. But then the car radio blares to life, and there's that CBC program about writers, there's the smooth-voiced host, so smart and interested, asking soulful deep questions to some writer . . . and off I go. Again.

Radio Host: You may recall my interview last year, at the Toronto Literary Festival with author Janet Mair about her wonderful novel, *Final Draft*. Mair's book, which critics and readers alike found funny, erotic and playful, describes a romance between a fiftyish Canadian woman writer and a famous male novelist from Britain. Welcome back to the studio, Janet Mair.

Hi.

Many readers have been struck by your fictional Leland Mackenzie's resemblance to a certain real British writer, multiple award winner and author of some of the finest novels

---

[3] Dear Reader: Remember that these downward arrows indicate Janet's fantasies, while sideways ones indicate that she's back in her real world, such as it is.

we have. The first question I want to ask is have you ever met this author?

Yes, we met informally when I was in London for a reading.

And?

And well, I sort of asked his permission to use his . . . likeness in my novel. And he agreed good humouredly. And that was that.

No sparks?

Heavens no!

None, Janet Mair?

Look, he's happily married, and I'm happily partnered. So no. No sparks.

I ask because there was quite a buzz at this year's festival. Both of you were slated to appear and there was tremendous interest in whether or not you would meet, even though you were scheduled to appear on different days. Were you in attendance at his readings or panels?

No. Yes. Well, some.

Were you ever in the same room at the same time at any of the social events or parties?

Not that I recall.

Well, there have been strange rumours. Even before the festival ended, a staffer let slip that the separation of your schedules had come at the British publisher's request.

I doubt that.

That it was written into his contract.

Weird.

A more bizarre rumour was that both of you were guests at the Toronto home of Canada's most famous literary couple. Stories surfaced of you two sneaking in through the alley

198

behind their home in The Annex, holding hands and necking like a couple of randy teenagers.

Don't you just love tabloid so-called journalism?

One other odd thing, though: I happened to be in London recently, and I noticed the teeniest item on the business page of the *Times* which mentioned some legal matter resolved in our famous author's divorce, thus clearing the way for the sale of foreign rights to his next bestseller-to-be. Did you know he got divorced?

No. Yes. Um.

I did some digging and found out that he filed for divorce last summer. And unlike many of the splashier Brit Lit marital bust-ups, this one was quiet, uncontested. And apparently very expensive.

Maybe so, but it's nothing to do with —

And then last summer the *Vancouver Sun* reported our author, famous and dishevelled, at a hardware store in Cranbrook, BC —

Saturday night, Matt's AWOL and Eric's at the wave pool with the neighbours. Aah, the house to myself. But no, Matt and his friends return and the rumble of skateboard wheels on the wooden deck, their harsh laughter and randy noise unsettle me, make me feel hunted. As usual, I seek sanctuary in my room. Then it occurs to me: it's Saturday night, Eric's safe, Matt's home, why do I need to stay here?

So I leave, with minimal explanation and little planning. It's only after I order my green tea at the coffee shop that I realize I'm broke, that I've handed over all my bills to Eric for the pool. The nice man at the counter lets me have my tea anyway, though. For seventy-six cents. The banality of my existence juxtaposed with these lush dreams. But how delicious, what happiness to be so immersed, so taken up, so carried away. I watch an elderly woman walk through the coffee bar. Neat shiny grey hair, well cut. A trim figure. Smooth skin.

Over and over, I tell myself that I'm too old for all this yearning. It's ridiculous. This morning, more signs: a white pearl of richly fertile mucous. If biology is destiny, it also has a weird sense of humour. Oh I know how this madness ends. I invented a new scene this morning. I tried it out before writing it, "imagined it out" as Eric would say. The boys were still asleep. I hope. And this new scene is spectacular. Just a slight revision in which ... *he has her prepared, secured, naked and has asserted himself through a few small teasing touches. He licks his finger and now he is ready but still he takes his time. He undresses very slowly* — does he say that line now? it's just a great line — *he stands silent at the foot of the bed, sipping his drink until she turns her head to look at him. Once he has her attention, he begins, with a maddening lack of haste, to undress, then he says —*

A burst of laughter from the beautiful old woman across the room, talking with her friends. Across the street, a man is climbing a ladder to fix a roof, his slim hips moving smoothly and surely in faded jeans.

The skateboarders are gone when I get home, Eric is in bed, happy and stinking of chlorine. There's a magazine in the bathroom, tossed on the floor alongside Matt's boxers, socks and T-shirt. I sit there, staring down at the back cover. At what appears to be an advertisement for socks. A very pretty blonde, naked, sits with her knees drawn up, hands draped just so, like the girl in that Ken Danby painting of the *Sunbather*. This position allows the pretty young naked blonde not only to conceal her breasts and crotch, but also to display the socks she is wearing. On one side of the ad are three smaller photographs of the same young woman, head shots only. It takes me a while to interpret these smaller pictures, as I sit on the can gazing at the back cover of the skateboarding magazine. The woman's head is on a pillow. The woman's face shows various stages of sexual pleasure. I realize that the photographer pretty well has to be stuck right up her at the moment the photos were taken. Or at least that's the illusion intended.

It shakes me, then, this most private passion on display — feigned, of course, but isn't that worse? — in order to sell socks. The image is somehow far more obscene than the juicy spreads that I know Matt keeps hidden under the mattress in his room, and as I sit here, I feel a tawdry shadow falling over whatever joy I might steal from the strange fever that has overtaken me these days.

I offer to help our hostess, the female half of Canada's most famous literary couple, with the dishes after the guys have headed off to an interview at CITYTV. It doesn't take long for her to exhaust the pleasantries and get to her point: "The re-creation of sexual passion is so much easier in poetry than novels. You can't really even fully remember physical pleasure, don't you think?"

"I agree it's one of the hardest things to write, certainly."

"Clean dishtowels in the end drawer, Janet. Have you had much reaction to the raunchy section of *Final Draft*?"

"Well, any copies I sent to elderly relatives had certain pages cut out." I expect a laugh here, but get only a grim smile.

"And your children?"

"I maintain my sanity in that regard by operating on the assumption that my kids have no interest at all in my books and that they never read them. It's worked pretty well for all of us, so far. How do you deal with questions around sexual content in your own work? The story about the mother, for example? Or that randy perverted doctor? The one who has an affair with his landlady?"

She turns toward me, her celebrated intense regard far more powerful and scary in person: "I would never, ever, use the abuse of sexual power as a narrative device."

I'm ready for this, though; holding her gaze, I say, "Neither would I. But desire's a pretty complicated thing, in my view. I read a *New Yorker* interview with Pauline Reage in which she dismissed *The Story of O* as an 'entertainment' she'd devised for a lover. She's an old woman now, can't understand what all the fuss was about."

"But she eroticizes male sadism and female masochism!"

"Yes, I suppose she does. O is 'a happy prisoner on whom everything is imposed and from whom nothing is asked.' On one level it's the female condition under patriarchy in a nutshell. In another sense it's a fantasy of abdication that I suspect has its attractions for every adult human on the planet. I mean, millions of copies of the story are in print, after all these years. I don't deny it's a dangerous fantasy but it's persistent, it's powerful, it has its seductions. And besides, millions of women also fantasize about extreme sexual power and domination. Different sides of the same coin, don't you think?"

"Possibly," my famous hostess says. "Cutlery drawer on the left."

Ray won't remember. I'd told him, of course, during our evening together, six weeks ago, before the fire, "I won't be back 'til Remembrance Day." I'd said it with some emphasis.

And I've forgotten about him, or nearly. Well, except for the thing that happened in the massage room, but that was just a blip. So today, going through the pass (leaving Calgary sunshine behind in the foothills, and driving into an inversion layer filling the mountain valleys with damp and cold) on the 11th of November, a Thursday, I idly think of Mister S in a generalized horny sort of way because I've got other men on my mind these days. There's that crazy guy I met online. And there's the man from election night, he's cute. Now poor old Leland, he's almost done, back on the shelf, for now. Worn out, used up, bless his heart.

So I hardly let Mister Sunshine cross my mind all the way down the highway. Except I decide that I'll call him when I arrive, or maybe just before I leave to come back home. Just to finish it off, put paid to it. Just a friendly, neutral, "Hi, how ya doin'? Back in the mountains for a few days, drop by for tea if you feel like it." Really, why not? A turn at bat consists of three strikes, right? So, before I left this morning, I fished his note — *call me anytime* — out of the phone file and tucked it into my wallet. More, I told myself, out of a desire to just put this one away than any hope of —

There's his van. I pull onto the ranch road, make the turn to the cabin, remember to say hello to the lake, and there's a flash of yellow at the next cottage over. His van. Mister Sunshine's. On November 11th. A holiday.

Now who could blame me? Who could blame me for letting my spirits soar, for letting it all come back in a rush? For thinking he has come for me? Who could blame me for entering the cabin and playing my latest pop infatuation, The Killers, really loud, and dancing in the living room? For thanking my lucky stars I'd thought to throw my best lingerie into the sports bag at the last moment? The signs are there, there is no other way to read them. Mister Sunshine has come for me, for Janet. For me.

I'm ready for his knock on the door by three. When he hasn't popped over — my car visible, the smoke from the chimney, the pounding beat of "Somebody Told Me" (sound carries so well out here on the lake) — I decide that it's time to take the dog for a walk. I look good; I've even risked a faint smudge of eye pencil and a swipe of lipstick, rubbed off with a Kleenex. Anathema to wear make-up at the lake, but this is a special day. Remembrance Day. He remembered.

The yellow van is parked beside the cottage a few hundred yards from ours. Stan's white pickup is there too. The two of them are inside, working together. I figure that I'll find them if I circle the house; they must be in a garage or basement that opens to the outside, like at my place. And this time, when I come upon them, I will not say something stupid. I will say the right thing. "Hi" seems like a good start. I will receive a warm smile of greeting; he is so glad to see me, he has hoped against hope that I'd come —

No luck. All the way around the house — no basement entrance, no garage — to peer in the sliding glass door on the lake side, but the drapes are closed tight. I knock at the front door, calling "Hello?" shyly, once then again, but there's not a sound from within, despite the fact of two vehicles parked in the drive. It occurs to me, right at that moment, that one of the things I love about Mister Sunshine is that, unlike 99 percent of the workmen I've encountered, he doesn't listen to classic rock FM radio while he works. I still remember having my basement painted by a ferret-faced man who was excruciatingly partial to Foreigner and Styx and Bryan Adams, and who tortured me with repeated renditions of "Hot Blooded."

The dog is bouncing, impatient, poking the backs of my legs, herding me down the road. I decide to just continue my walk. I'll stop by again on the way back. The road is a mile long oval, running along the lakeshore, then circling back up through the trees above the hayfield. I'm so happy, rehearsing the ecstatic news to Paula — yes, the drought has ended, praise the lord — when I hear something behind me, just as I reach the far end of the loop. It's Stan, in his white pickup. Out of politeness, he stops. Out of politeness, I ask him about his arthritis, and his answer is anxious, pained, befuddled and excessively detailed. Once he runs down, I ask, "So, you were just over . . . next door, were you?"

"Oh. Yeah. I bin workin' with that, what's his name, installing the water system. Ray."

Exultation. No doubt. Not an underling or subcontractor or crew. Just him. He came for me. Mister Sunshine. I extricate myself from Stan's dismay at the state of his knees and fairly dance down the road. I do not rush, though, or try not to, try to keep the pace measured and steady. Take my time, savour it. It's going to happen, and not just in my head this time. He has come for me.

I make the final turn and head back toward the cabin. The neighbour's roof is in sight now. It's too perfect that Stan's gone, it'll just be the two of us. Mister Sunshine and me. "Hi" still seems like a good enough start. There are the walls of the neighbour's cabin. The van's roof should be visible by the time I can see those; did he move it?

The van is gone. This does not distress me. He's probably waiting out in front of my place. The yellow roof of his van will come into view any second —

But the only car in front of the cabin is my own. My spirits don't flag, though, not in the slightest. Isn't this funny, how could we have missed each other like this? He's just finished up and followed Stan down the road to do up the invoice or put some tools away or maybe to take some debris to the dump. He has knocked at my door, of course, puzzled that I didn't answer; or perhaps he's called, no answering machine at the cabin, no way. So he'll be over any minute now. I poke the fire. Then, just in case, dig the slip of paper out of my wallet and, without taking even a second to talk myself into it, call his cell number. He answers on the second ring.

"Hi Ray. This is Janet. Janet Mair?" I'm so sure, still.

"Oh. Janet, hi. How are you?"

"Great thanks, but it looks like I just missed you. Saw your van parked next door and then after I got back from walking the dog, it was gone. How weird is that? I even came by the

206

house to say hi, but I couldn't find you. You haven't finished work over there for the day, have you?"

"Well, yeah, just now. You mean you're there? God, I must be blind. And I even asked Stan if anyone was up for the long weekend and he said, 'No, nobody's here.' Oh man. So you're there. I can't believe I missed you."

"Oh well. No sweat. So where are you right now?" He can't be more than ten minutes down the road. He could turn around right now, this minute.

"On my way to the next job. A really ugly job that I just want to get rid of — "

"But it's a holiday. I mean, I was just hoping you might be able to drop by. For tea or something. It would be good to see you."

"Yeah, typical me, didn't even twig that it's a holiday. So how long are you here?"

"Not sure. I did try to get my kids to come, but they bitched and whined and I finally said, okay fine, if you can find yourselves a place to stay. So I'm here on my own again, just working away on this manuscript . . . 'til Saturday morning for sure. Maybe Sunday, depending on how things go."

I've already decided that, once the wild scenes I imagine get rolling in real life, no flippin' way I'm going to want to set foot out the door until Sunday, nor will he let me.

"Well," says Ray, says Mister S. "Hmm, let me think. That could work, I guess. I probably won't be going to the city this weekend."

He's been coming to the city? on weekends?

I say, "It'd be good to see you. Just give me a call, okay? Do you have the number?"

"Right here on my phone." He repeats it back to me.

"That's the one. Well. Good luck with the job from hell."

"Thanks. Talk to you soon, then."

When I replay the call in my mind later on, which I am given ample time to do, I try to remember exactly what I'd said next. Did I sound eager or indifferent? Did I actually say "no pressure" or "whatever" or do I just think I did?

I spend that Thursday evening watching the fire. A flattering sweater, a hint of colour on eyes and lips. Pubes freshly trimmed, amazing how sensitive that little exposure makes me, thighs and between tingling, mouth wanting to open, sweet scenes in my head, cheeky banter, passion's throes, the heat cranking up higher and higher, for weeks now.

I even went online last month on a dare from Paula. Met a guy for coffee. An ex-army guy, forty-seven, now working in aircraft repair. New grandfather of a two-month-old boy. His daughter is twenty, lives in Sherwood Park. He was married twice. An amateur photographer. He very proudly showed me a local magazine for which he'd done the photos. I must remember to show the mag to someone, Paula or Manjini, so they'd know who to look for if I get stalked or murdered or abducted. And okay, okay, I should have pulled up short at his persistence. During the cyber courtship, he emailed twice a day, very keen to meet. Once I'd agreed, the pressure let up. We met at a coffee shop on a weekday, after my workout. And he seemed like an okay guy. Small, wiry — his parents escaped Hungary in 1956, just before the revolution. Attila — yes, his name was Attila, Paula nearly busted a gut over that — he talked quite charmingly of his travels as a peacekeeper, talked politics, kids, gardens. He insisted on buying my tea, and afterwards toured me through an art gallery that really did have some neat stuff in it, by Evan Penny: the ordinary human made grotesque, rendered surreal. So perhaps I let my guard down a bit. I'd been careful to call him only from a cell, and had given him a fake name. But then he was so little and cute and obviously keen that I gave him a hug when we said goodbye on the street. And he was very pleased by this, and very responsive. I wasn't thinking straight, and I let him follow me to my car. Only later did I wonder whether he'd gotten my licence plate down. So I hopped inside, eager now to get away, said, "I'll be in touch." By that evening, there was an email headed Hello Gorgeous which, okay, okay, did my heart good. God, how long has it been since anyone said that to me? I remember last summer, sitting at the pub waiting for Paula to arrive, and seeing a man enter, look around, then stride over to a woman waiting for him at the bar, kiss her and say, "Hello, beautiful." It made my heart ache. But this guy, this Attila, was — I don't know — pretty intense. So I wrote him back a couple of days later, told him my circumstances have changed, I've met someone, nice to meet you, best of luck. You're a nice guy.

He wrote back: Maybe I am a nice guy but it don't seem to do me much good.

Hours pass, before the fire. My cute lines about only having meatloaf sandwiches to offer Ray this time become tiresome, and by eight, the wine bottle empty, the merest thought of meatloaf makes me want to gag, so I microwave a Lean Cuisine, which I shovel down my throat without enjoyment, just plugging the hole. Questions arise. How could he have missed seeing my car? You can't miss it, there's a clear view of my driveway from the neighbour's gate.

And why would Stan have said there's no one here? He knew I was coming up today, I'd called ahead to tell him so. Being protective or something, in league with Dad Moe to protect my infuriating virtue? He was there when I invited Ray for tea last September, maybe he saw Ray's van there late that night. Fuck Stan, meddling old prick.

Because I knew I'd be confronting one last time the dissolution of the affair between Leland and Jay this weekend, the letting go, I've brought sad music — masses, requiems, chant. Despair flirts around the edges of this vast pulsing sticky wad of need, of foolish hope and obscene dreams, dances around it like the blue dervishes of flame that twirl and twist, rise and recede, against the bark of each new log. I just observe them, these dervishes, with benign interest. I know. He came for me. What other explanation could there possibly be? My back hurts, though. I take a couple of painkillers, deliberately forgetting to remember that this particular combination of drugs and alcohol lets me sleep, but leaves me depressed as hell the next day.

I can't stop this. Now I'm in London, with the Englishman, the man who inspired Leland, in a pub before my reading the next day. The novel has been a huge success, and the Englishman has agreed to meet, to "give his blessing" is what he has said. After a drink, we stroll to a park bench.

He raises my hand to his lips and I start to cry: "I — oh god — I took that part out of the book because it was too corny. Too romantic."

"I must have missed it," he murmurs, "wished it were there, I guess," and offers me a handkerchief. We sit together in the park. We like each other, a lot. My left hand strays to his leg. I grab it, slap it with the right — "bad hand, no!" — and he laughs. Gently frees the hand and sets it on his pant leg, covered by his own. Other arm around my shoulders. A kiss. Aaah.

Well —

Back to my hotel and it's like the scene in *Jane Eyre* where Rochester's saying goodnight after Jane saves him from the fire but he won't let go of her hand.

Maybe I pull him along or maybe he follows after a moment.

and and and

well, yes.

But as he dresses to leave I ask him, "So what are you going to do about the pictures?"

"Pardon?"

"The photographs of us on the bench, the kiss. You walking into my hotel with your hand on my butt. You looking out the window of my room, with your chest bare."

He sits down, heavily, on the edge of the bed. "I've made a mistake."

"What I don't get — actually, two things: first, what are the photos for? Blackmail? Or just publicity? I'm a small town girl, I don't really understand how the real world works — "

"Look — "

211

"And the second question: why did you fuck me? You didn't have to."

His look of pain might make me feel sorry for him, if I weren't so humiliated. He mutters, "I have spent thirty years — "

"You could've just said no. To my query letter, to this meeting, to . . . all of it. I gave you the option, over and over."

Angry now, he stands. "Look. I have spent thirty years building a reputation, and if you think a little snip nobody's ever heard of can just waltz in and take what's mine — "

The fog settles in over the lake and Friday goes on forever. In the morning I manage a little work, editing some of the email banter between Leland and Jay, but as the day wears on and hope wears thin, I'm paralyzed, drawn to the chair before the fire, to sad songs. Amazing how even in this dry mountain air, even with the heat of the hearth drawing every drop of moisture from my body, I can still cry so much. I must remember to keep my fluids up though; I'm hungover enough from the wine and the pills.

I don't get it. Or perhaps I do. Remembrance Day is over, after all, and out of nowhere, I remember, a few years ago, passing a couple of young guys outside Safeway. Overhearing one say to the other, "So I told her if she didn't lose some weight, I was leaving her. I just wanted to see what she'd do."

That's what this kid said: *I just wanted to see what she'd do.*

That quick lie of Ray's — yes, of course it was a lie — about going off to another job, at that time of day. How could Mister Sunshine be a liar? How could he have sat there on the couch before the fire six weeks ago and talked of his daughter and his life and his father's illness and dancing at Shambala and how he likes being a man and believes in intuition and yet be so smooth in a lie?

By midnight, I have it clear. As I circled the neighbour's house yesterday afternoon, wearing my flattering mauve sweater, with my smudge of deep blue eyeliner, with my trimmed pubes, as I shyly called "Hello?" outside the silent house, the two men stood conspiratorially inside. Huddled together, stifling laughter. Stan's in on it of course — the brotherhood. Ray has said, "You gotta help me out here," and the two of them exchange mischievous glances when they peer through the closed curtains and see that I have walked away. To heighten the joke, Ray then sends Stan down the road in his pickup, to make sure I know. That Ray is there, that he's alone in the neighbour's house. For Ray, the best part is booting it up the road before I can walk the last half of the loop; he smiles to himself, picturing my quick eager stride, my expectant smile. He hasn't told Stan why he booked this job for the 11th, though. He hasn't told Stan that he scheduled things this way because *he just wanted to see what I'd do.*

When I was a kid, my mother hid the back issues of Dad's *Playboy* magazines in a high cupboard in the laundry room. There was a recurring cartoon figure in those glossy pages: the lusty little old lady. Grey hair in a bun, spectacles, scrawny little body and pendulous sagging boobs. In every joke she is frustrated and disappointed, virile young men fleeing her advances with a mixture of terror and disgust. What could be more repulsive, more absurd, than a horny old woman?

That's a sad story. Here's another. Last Sunday, I went for a massage. I usually find the treatments very relaxing, even come close to falling asleep on the table while Liz works her mysterious magic on my poor crooked little body. I hadn't been for a treatment for months though, not since the awakening. But this time, instead of just relaxing and falling asleep, I plunged fathoms deep into a fantasy about being naked with Ray. Odd that it was Ray, definitely Ray. But never mind. All this time, ever since the last bleed, I've just stayed very juicy, because I like it and it's a nice change. And I hold the image in my mind of a beautiful hard circumcised cock, beautiful shapely head like a medieval helmet. The cock is very long and very hard, angled up. And I keep myself juiced, have done for months now, by imagining that cock going into me. I also picture strong hands grasping my hips, moving me back and forth on that marvellous cock, and sometimes above, faintly, I picture a man's dark head, features unclear but a look that is merely serious and intent.

That image mutated into Ray that day on the table in Liz's little lavender-scented massage room. His cock was beautiful. The whole session, ninety minutes, was just . . . oh, man. I took him in my mouth over and over. He entered me with serious purpose, over and over. I was red hot, I was miles away, ecstatic, wet, swollen. In so deep I feared I'd never come out again. I hope I didn't moan. I really worried about Liz, such a funny shy woman who lives alone with her cats and has a troublesome mother and whose little hands warm and heal as if by magic. I worried she'd tune in to this energy somehow and just get, I don't know, blasted across the room.

Late Friday night, cried out, I sit before the dying fire and page listlessly through an old *Utne Reader* that Paula left behind. I find an article about a woman in her fifties, happily married, who became fixated on a young man she'd met on a hiking trip. The woman wrestled with this infatuation, but ended up recognizing it as a larger lust, the call not of sex or romance but of something she learned to call her Inner Beloved: the soul of the world asking to love her and be loved by her.

I think about this, for a while. Remembering that moment on the deck, back in August, the opening up. Maybe.

But then I decide, *ah, fuck my inner beloved. I just wanna get laid.*

So there's Ray, right now, at his parents' place, a few miles away. He wears a secret smile. He knows where I am, right now. He can picture what I'm doing. All through dinner, he keeps his secret smile, and afterwards, he helps his mom lift and turn his dad, helps her clean the bedsores, check the dressings, adjust the morphine drip.

Saturday morning, I'm on the road before dawn. I've hardly noticed that I was in the mountains: all that beauty and peace unremarked, muffled in fog. I keep thinking that I'm cried out, but surprise myself over and over. A bloody hunk of roadkill, a stray thought, a pop tune like "Free Fallin'" and I'm off again, blurry, wet, a road menace. What is it gonna take? I wonder.

I wish I could tell Ray what a good time I would've shown him. After I did myself last night, second time that day, I laughed and muttered, "Suckerrr, you missed out on something amazing." And he did. He missed out on me. Janet.

215

Janet Mair. Mother writer woman teacher human being. I don't know how it has happened, but it's perfectly clear to me now that I have somehow become the sort of woman who only stupid and/or crazy men want to fuck. If I meet someone I can actually have a conversation with, he's not interested. I get hit on by stupid men all the time.

Back home Saturday midday. House still standing, kids alive. So far so good. Eric wants to go for a sleepover at his buddy's place. Great idea, I say. So I'm in my office, listening to REM. I have Ray's cheery note, with his numbers. *call me anytime*

I have a plate. I have matches. Let the ceremony begin.

Ritual completed, and Saturday night looms. Matt's at home tonight, hunched over the computer. I'm too tired for anything, ready to put my nightie on by 5:30, but I force myself to wait 'til at least seven, when it's dark. What was life like before this delirium, what thoughts and hopes and nightmares? I can't even remember, but am nostalgic anyway for the simplicity of whatever it might have been — any pain but this pain.

I rented a documentary called *Gambling, Gods and LSD* for the trip, but didn't watch it — too busy crying — and decide to try it now. The director, Peter Mettler, begins with the manic ugliness of Toronto's airport strip, the crass promise of the fantasy penthouse at the Constellation, then the bizarre antics of a Christian revival meeting — no, prior to that a recovering heroin addict who sucks life from a cigar, says he still misses the kick, still longs for the kick. Then Mettler moves to Los Alamos, and after that Las Vegas, where a slick man proudly shows off his Fantasy Museum — lifeless mannequins in leather and chains, a dildo so startlingly reminiscent of the cock of my dreams that I blush with shame. By the time Mettler's camera moves inside a peep show booth, I am suddenly aware that my teenage son sits nearby at the computer, headphones blasting Nine Inch Nails, engrossed in *Counter-Strike*, his violent and powerful fantasy.

I turn off my video and go to bed, paging through the books piled there, prep for a novel I'm teaching that's set in postwar Europe. According to the *Cambridge History of Germany*, in the GDR, the Reds re-used the Buchenwald infrastructure to torture and kill anti-communists by the tens of thousands. They even used ex-Nazi thugs as hired help; the guys required no training at all. And in *Walking Since Daybreak*, Modris Eksteins describes how the Russians regarded murder, looting, and rape as legitimate tools for the crushing of fascism. Stalin, when questioned on this point, replied with irritation, "Can't he understand it if a soldier who has crossed thousands of kilometers through blood and fire and death has fun with a woman or takes some trifle?" And in Marcia Davenport's *Too Strong For Fantasy*, the hideous hunger for power destroys love, destroys hope, destroys justice, steals Jan Masaryk and his father's dream, turns the world again and always to shit to shit to shit.

Tears. An endless supply today, apparently. Mucous blocks my nose, I gasp for breath. When I finally stumble out of my room in search of more Kleenex, I realize that, down the hall in the family room, my son has the headphones off, can hear me. I get dressed, grab the car keys. "Can't sleep, Matt. Going for a drive, okay?"

"Hope it makes you feel better, Mom."

I drive. The way the tears blur the neon is kind of pretty. After an hour and a half, I stop at a drive-thru and I remember — this is remembrance weekend after all — to notice the trim young man working the window. To register, acknowledge, that this is how he is spending his Saturday night because there are things he needs and wants and he is willing to work this job to get them. And back at home, Matt is grateful for the cheeseburger combo I've brought him. Only then does it occur to me to wonder why he too is home alone on a Saturday night.

Oh I have ta'en too little care of this.

Dare I accuse Ray of deliberate cruelty or is that just my own fever dream? More likely mere carelessness. Or indifference. Likely all Ray's guilty of is a few awkward lies (he realizes he shouldn't have led me to believe he's single, and now is caught in a trap of his own devising) or even fear (I'm too hungry, too serious, I scare the shit out of him, I'll eat him alive). Not malice, just ambivalence. Which is worse? Malice certainly feels less humiliating.

While Matt finishes his burger at the kitchen table, I wander out onto the deck, look at the stars. Far fewer than the night, less than two months ago, when I stood at the gate with Ray. It occurs to me all over again that I am no longer the kind of woman that a sane man lunges at. And age isn't the only reason for that. I tell myself, "Janet, you are no longer a dish. You are too opinionated. You do not please, anymore. You have forgotten how to please, and, admit it, even if you remembered how, you probably couldn't be bothered. So from here on in, you really have to fucking insist. You have to draw a diagram." And I understand, finally, that that's exactly where *Final Draft* goes wrong, is dishonest. Because Leland reaches for Jay in that hotel room in Toronto the night they meet. That rings false. That would not happen.

I lie in bed, drifting, trying to sleep. And in my waking dream, the doorbell rings, and it's Ray —

No.

I sleep, finally. And in my dream, the doorbell does ring. But it is not Leland, nor is it the man he stands in for. It's not Ray, either. No. It's the peacekeeper. It's Attila.

And in my terrible dream, while my son lies sleeping in his basement lair, among his posters of Tony Hawk and Hilary Duff, dreaming his dreams of the perfect head shot, of something hard and sharp in a hot wet place, I, his mother, surrender to a great passion. I never even get a glimpse of what might have been the cock of my dreams. No. Just the kind strength of Attila's hands.

"Janet," the Englishman says, "tell me. Why do you want to publish this book?"

"All the usual reasons. Ego, greed, certainly. But also the simple desire to be heard, to know that maybe what I think, what I've noticed, matters. To give pleasure. To show what I've learned. To please the reader, to please myself."

He says, "Gerard Manley Hopkins just wrote for himself. And for God."

219

"Yes, and so did Emily Dickinson — the two litmus tests of writerly virtue, I know, I know. But I'm not that pure. And neither are you."

It's unseasonably warm for late November, and my Canlit seminar votes to move outside for the last half of the class. I sit yoga fashion on the ground near the flagpole, a few students share the only wooden bench, and the rest sprawl on the dry grass. We're wrapping up our discussion of Margaret Laurence's *The Diviners*.

The dreadlocked guy furrows his brow, says, "So you mean that her husband, that professor guy, kinda represents colonialism?"

"Well, sort of. I guess I'm suggesting that Laurence quite deliberately makes Morag's romantic life a mirror of her writing life, her creative life. Morag marries her English professor, Brooke Skelton, whose own brokenness, by the way, is associated with imperialism. You'll recall his account of being raised under the Raj in India. But that union is barren, unequal, doomed. Contrast that with Morag's relationship with Jules Tonnerre, which is erratic and uncertain and ultimately tragic, but it does bear fruit, namely their daughter Piquette. And it's fruitful because the relationship is grounded not in some externally imposed notion of cultural identity, but in the very native soil where Morag was born and raised."

Renee raises her hand, excited. "So it's the same with her writing, you mean? That if she focuses on her own stuff instead of trying to imitate some kind of canonical notion of what literature is, then she succeeds?"

"Yes, exactly. I think you're right," I tell her. And shy little Renee just beams.

After class, I stop off in the mailroom on my way out and notice the balding head of one of my least favourite colleagues, too late to duck back down the hall. He's the one I used as the prototype for the fawning co-worker of Jay's who accosts her and Leland on campus that day of the surprise visit to the college where she teaches. "Class good today?" he asks, and for something to say, I mention how my whole Canlit group initially bitched and whined about having to read *The Diviners:* "'It's so LONG,' they wailed, their eyes bugging out. Why the hell do they sign up for English classes if they don't want to *read*? But I'm pleased to report that they seemed totally into it by the time we wrapped things up today."

"Ah yes, good old Morag," the man says, leering. "A very lusty woman." As I walk away, I'm thinking, No. No, he's wrong, that's not it at all, she's not lusty. She's normal. It's what I've always loved about her. The frankness of her desire. The novel isn't a dirty joke and anyone who reads it as one has totally missed the point. As I walk away, it occurs to me that Jay makes much the same journey, with Leland, as Morag does with Brooke.

Leaving the building, I catch up with Renee. She's a pale, kind of doughy girl, huddled around her binders and textbooks. I come up behind her and say, "I was sure pleased to see you getting into the discussion today."

"Oh yes," she says, softly. "This class, this whole term, I sort of feel like the world is opening up in some way. That *this* is

221

connected to *that*, and this thing is a reference to that thing and it's so, I don't know. Cool, I guess."

"Yes. To see the assumptions behind the structures of things is kind of empowering, isn't it? If you can see how it's built then you can see your way through it somehow."

"Yes, exactly!" she exclaims, with a sudden warmth that surprises me. I get the feeling she would throw her arms around me if she dared. But of course, she doesn't dare.

Still, it's a tender moment. One that reminds me why I love teaching. And on my way home, in traffic, on Deerfoot Trail, it occurs to me to ask myself, *Where have I been? What's the point of all this sturm und drang when all the tenderness I crave is right here in front of me if I only have eyes to see it?*

That night, after supper and homework and dishes, I go down to my basement office and pull the manuscript out of the drawer. Grab a piece of lined paper and hand write a letter to my agent. "I know it's been a while, but here's the novel I've been working on. It's called *Final Draft*. Let me know what you think."

A LUCID DREAM REVISITED

"I'm being totally honest," I say. I always am and they know it. There's no point in being anything else, is the way I look at it, and sooner or later the truth will out so you might as well not waste the time, right?

"Rape Fantasies" from *Dancing Girls and Other Stories*
Margaret Atwood

Reader, she invented them. Jay, Leland, Janet, Mister Sunshine. All of them.

JM did, I mean. She released a novel called *A Happy Prisoner* and it sank like a stone.

Or maybe people loved it, and it won a gazillion awards.

Doesn't matter.

Reader, she invented him. Like Charlotte Bronte invented Rochester, made him difficult and often cruel. Made him atone, too, humbled him. Now our JM, she doesn't play that way, or maybe she's too wise. She just had to let Leland be.

Charlotte invented a lover with whom conversation was 'audible thinking.' And then in real life she married the Reverend Arthur Nichols, after everyone she loved had died. She herself died within a year of her marriage. From "complications of pregnancy."

On the other hand, JM is past childbearing. That's something to keep in mind.

Suppose she did actually meet him, though. *Him.* The Englishman. The one on whom Leland is based.

See, in October, when she's gazing at a review, sipping coffee, watching light snow drifting off roofs under the bright blue Calgary sky, she gets this call from an agent in the U.K. Plummy accent, says he wants her to meet him in the lobby lounge at the Westin, next Thursday at three, to talk about a potential contract.

She enters the near-empty bar and sits on a banquette, facing outwards. Orders a drink, and a dark-haired man rises from his barstool, approaches her. "Waiting for someone?"

Oh god, it's him. "You set me up, didn't you?"

A nod. He reaches into his jacket, laughing when she flinches. He murmurs, "Don't be afraid of me. I promise I won't hurt you."

"Hey," she shoots back, without thinking, "write your own goddamn dialogue!"

He grins. "Don't quote yourself. It's arrogant. It's unseemly." The object he'd been reaching for is the paperback edition of her book. "I was hoping you'd sign this for me."

"You came all the way here for this?"

"I've been doing some research in Vancouver. This is just a stopover."

Blushing, she searches her bag for a pen. "So," she says, "you're all right with all of this, then?"

"Of course. It isn't me you laid bare, after all. And it wasn't you who wrote the novel, right? That was Janet."

"So you thought you'd just stop by to point that out?"

"And to see how you're doing," he says. "How are you doing?"

"Well, on the one hand, I'm in constant peril of turning into an asshole. And on the other, I feel so exposed and embarrassed I could just fucking die."

"That sounds about right. One question more?"

"All right."

"What, exactly, is the five-hole?"

So perhaps they had a drink and talked about writing. And his flight was at six, so they just barely had time for a walk with the dog on her own little acre of urban prairie. (He knows what prairie means, by the way.) But if he was struck by something he saw there, some vision or memory, he didn't mention it.

At the airport, she reached up and rested her hand on the side of his face, and planted a shy kiss on the other. But she didn't say the line, "You're way better than the man I imagined," because she knew not to fall in love with her own good lines. She couldn't think what else to say though, so she settled for, "Thanks for the ambush." To which he replied, "One good turn deserves another." Then he turned and walked through the gate.

Yes, she's caught in this dream, JM is; she can't stop this dreaming.

I can't stop this dream —

In her real life, JM met this man whose teeth didn't match. After they'd known each other a few weeks, he invited her to dinner at his place out in the country, near Water Valley.

The morning of the dinner, in anticipation, she grabbed a pack of Trojans at the Esso, from Dee, who sells her coffee and smokes every day.[4] Unable to ignore the question in Dee's eyes, she muttered, "Teenagers."

---

[4] Once when JM came to the till with coffee, jujubes, and potato chips, then asked for a pack of smokes, Dee commented, "Ah, good. You've got all the food groups."

"Ah," said Dee. "There was a young guy in here last week who wanted a pack of these but didn't have quite enough money. So I made up the difference for him. And then this woman in line behind him just tore a strip off me afterwards, but I said, 'Look, if it were my kid, I'd want somebody to help him out.' I mean, with my daughter — "

(Yes, the one with cleavage lavishly displayed front and back for a morning of junior high math? No kidding, JM thinks, still bristling at the realization that she can't even buy a condom in this town without having to explain.)

But oh, the luxurious preparations for that evening, that dinner in the country . . . choosing a shirt that will come off attractively and easily. Jeans that fit but are not so tight that they leave marks on the skin. And also loose enough to allow a hand. The lovely rituals of preparing the skin, the exfoliant scrub, the scented lotion; how long has it been since she has thought of such things? Too long.

But their first night together stunned her, a sweet derangement. His hands on her, so present yet so utterly strange. The unexpected nipple ring. The novelty of being gently warned about it.

When she slipped away before sunrise, leaned over to kiss him, his hair was lank with sweat against his neck. Strange how her writer self knows that fiction lies when it tells us that consummation concludes the narrative. Because, oh, this is so much more complicated than she thought it would be: no happy ending, merely a door opening onto a labyrinth, a pathless forest. The sea is *not* calm tonight.

She phoned him the day after, and the call went about as badly as it possibly could. The distance in his voice, the faint murmur, "Sure, yeah, let's get together again sometime soon." She doesn't know what to do, how to play this. She wants to speak her heart but doesn't dare.

oh his hands on me, his mouth

She thought things would be so straightforward, that she had imagined this event so fully that nothing could surprise her. But what caught her up was how real it was, how it felt, how it smelled, how it sounded . . . and oh god the love. She'd forgotten about that, the love. She thought of him constantly for days, flesh remembering the sweep of eager hands. There's so much to learn about this man. He cries out in his sleep. And the love: you can't even begin to imagine it.

POSTSCRIPTS

Jay: a dream come true

That first night we spent together, I told Leland a lot of things, but never this dream, one that I had over and over again before I met him. The dream unfolds on a cobblestone street in an ancient town, not a city, somewhere in Europe. I am older, in my seventies, wearing a long filmy gown, a flowing India print perhaps, cool and comfortable and appropriate for the season and the place. I am walking along with a man I've known a long time, taking him to my home for a visit. We are, for the first time in years, at peace with each other. My partner has died. But I am at peace.

When I first glimpsed this cobblestone street in my dreams, I thought that the man beside me was my ex-husband, the father of my children. But in truth, he did not live to be an old man, he was too careless for that. When the street first appeared in my dreams, I didn't even know Leland, and though I'd met Gray, I didn't like him very much at all. And after that first night with Leland, I never dreamed that dream again, not once. Funny how things turn out.

When the dream comes true, it's Leland and me, walking slowly, stately, through these ancient streets together, toward the modest little house where Gray lived out his final years with me. Leland and I sit together outside on the little beflowered deck that overlooks the sea, in the cool sunshine and salt breeze. I am wearing a long filmy dress of local manufacture, in soft fabric and soft colours. I have always wanted to dress like a gypsy and at last I can. Leland and I have a glass together and a quiet meal at the cafe down the road. And at bedtime (which comes at dusk, because we both are old) we embrace without passion and retire to our separate bedrooms. He is self-conscious about the bag concealed beneath the waistband of his trousers, and I of the diagonal scar where my breast used to be. But in the night I leave the bed I shared with Gray and pad barefoot down the hall to him, to Leland. And nestle against him like I used to, so many years ago.

230

Janet: a daydream

Mister Sunshine finally called a few days before Christmas as she was preparing a bath. Was contrite, said, "I didn't know what to do. I didn't expect to like you so much. I had this kind of porno fantasy about some rich bored housewife and I just — it was as if I couldn't reconcile what I'd imagined with what I actually encountered."

Janet listened, holding the phone to her ear, remembering the night she'd had dinner at the cabin with him, how she'd gestured to the piles of manuscript pushed to one side of the table, saying, "Yes, it's a novel I'm working on. And it's like a relationship in that I'm at the stage where the initial infatuation is over, and now I actually have to say, 'okay this is gonna work or it isn't' and go on to the next stage. The next draft."

She thanked Ray for the call, wished him a Merry Christmas and hung up the phone. She continued with her bath. It was late; Eric in bed, Matthew out with his girlfriend. She lay in the tub — the citrus verbena aroma of bath salts, the minor key of a Bach Adagio on the boombox, the glow of tea lights, her own body, its curves and furrows and blemishes and smoothness, its beauty and imperfection. What was missing that night, for probably the first time she could remember, was the male watcher in her mind, the one who admires and comments, who praises and disapproves. He didn't show up that night, and she didn't miss him at all. She was just there in the bath, her ownself, her own body. Just Janet and no one else.

231

JM: a lucid dream

I wrote to him, reader. I'm sure you know by now who I mean. The Englishman, the real writer. And he was lovely. A few emails back and forth, then he suggested a phone conference over "a few details" before he would be willing to grant me permission. Permission? To use — not him, exactly — but suggestions of his identity, in the published book. Time zones were troublesome; my weekday mornings too busy for his afternoons, and by the time I got a break in the action in Calgary, it would be after midnight where he lived. So we settled on a Saturday morning: I was to await his call between nine and nine-thirty.

So I've got the coffee on, kids still asleep. I should not have been surprised when the bell that rang was the front door.

I'd been anticipating the voice; now add the grey eyes and the sly smile and well . . . a miracle I got any words out at all. What I managed was, "You bastard! You set me up!"

"Ah," he said, "the famous flannelette nightie, the tent. I just had to see it with my own eyes."

I opened the door, set him to work making tea for himself while I dressed and combed my hair, then we sat side by side at the dining room table.

He brought his own copy of the galleys, flagged with post-its, plenty of notes in the margins. He made maybe eight or ten really potent technical points, and I was scribbling like mad, trying to get it all down. Then he said, "Now to the rather more thorny question of content."

"Please," I said, "tell me that all of your children are alive and well. That if you do have a mistress, she doesn't have piercings and dreads. That you're not going to punch me out — or Jay out, rather — for not liking your best book."

"Thank you, my children are thriving. My love life will not be adversely affected in any way. And as to the other, well. Everyone is entitled to her opinion, no matter how stupid."

"I'm glad."

"No, it's this. Here. About the sled. This troubles me. I have wracked my brain about it. I cannot understand how you got this."

"How I got it?"

"This is not public, never has been. I can say with absolute certainty that I have never told this story to a single journalist, ever. A few people close to me, perhaps, but — it matters to me how you found this out. All of us want, I think, to hold back just a few things, in order to keep some of measure of dignity, privacy, sanity even."

"Jesus — "

"Oh my." He registered it then, the look of shock on my face.

"I . . . gave it to you, to Leland I mean, but it's mine. It is. That's where I got it. Jay was just yakking away and I needed something for Leland so I gave him the sled story, but it's mine. It happened to me. When I was little. Though I made up the stitches."

"Well."

"Did you have stitches?"

"Yes. Twelve. This is very — "

"Yes it is."

He leaned back in his chair, rubbed his eyes. "Strange."

We fell silent for a while. Then I said, "Listen. There really is a place called Richdale. Could I show it to you? I could take you there. It's where my imagination comes from. I want you to see it. It's about a six-hour drive. We could get there before nightfall, but we'd have to stay over in the next town and come back tomorrow. Could you delay your flight? Just for a day?"

He hesitated only a moment. "Yes. I believe I could."

The phone calls and child care arrangements and dog-feeding instructions were accomplished in just over an hour and we were on our way. We talked very little in the car. The landscape seemed to mesmerize him; he murmured, "Where I come from, a six-hour drive ends you up in Italy."

"Well here it just barely gets you into the next province."

It's a raw day, the wind is chilly, and dusk is threatening to fall as we pull into Richdale. I show him the sledding hill first, then what's left of the town. The cemetery comes last, just as the light begins to go. We take our time, wandering separately in the small enclosure. He wants to see everything, take everything in. He finds the solitary stone inscribed for "wee Mary" that kicked my first novel into being. It's over in a windswept corner, and he crouches and runs his hands over the blackened lettering.

I just watch him, mostly. Smelling the sage kicked up by the wind. 'til he finally straightens, tries to pinpoint the horizon. Then he walks over to where I am standing. I bend down, pick a sprig of sage from the earth at my feet. "Hold out your hand," I say and press it into his palm, close his hand over it and twist it in my own to crush the buds. "Now smell."

He raises his hand to his face and opens it, inhales. I see it in his eyes. He gets it, now. He knows what I know. The wind's cold. I shiver, move toward him. "Put your arms around me . . . please." And he steps close, lifting his hand above my head, as if blessing me. Lets the crushed sage fall, works it into my hair with his fine white hands, then he pulls me close to his chest in the raw wind.

And perhaps, just perhaps, a trucker barrelling down the highway that evening glanced over into the graveyard, and what he saw was a woman standing there all alone. Tossing her head back and laughing with joy, then dancing and waving her arms in the wind. All by herself in the waning light. And maybe he thought to himself, "Crazy broad, headcase." So what?

APPENDIX # 1:
A PLACE AT THE TABLE

In which the Author replies to her critics, with
footnotes.

DISCLAIMER:
ALL OF THIS IS COMPLETELY TRUE

Scene One: Interior. Day. Coffee shop at a small college. Zoom in to a table occupied by a group including Man of Letters and several young people, all of whom appear to be vying for the attention of M of L.

Young Woman: So, what are you going to do once term ends and you're rid of the gang of us? Go back to being a Major Canadian Novelist?

M of L: Probably stare at my hands a lot and fall into a deep depression.

Young Man: When is your next book coming out anyway?

Scene Two: Exterior. Day. Woman of Letters hurries to catch up to Man of Letters, who is walking ahead of her. We see her get his attention and engage him in conversation, but can't hear what's being said at first, until the camera zooms closer.

W of L: I mean, after my friend read it, she gave me this look and said, "It's great to see this kind of thing being said by a middle-aged woman. I mean, this is the kind of fantasy a man would write." So that got me interested in finding out what a man would think of it.

M of L: I suppose I could read it if you like.

W of L: Well, thanks, I appreciate this. Wow, look at those iris. Amazing, huh.

M of L: (stretches, squints, almost grimaces) I guess so.[5]

Scene Three: Interior. A faculty office. Papers and books scattered everywhere. Woman of Letters on the phone.

---

[5] "The inability to appreciate flowers is a sign of clinical depression." *The Botany of Desire.*

W of L: So. I got his critique today. He left it in my mailbox.

Voice from phone, male: So, what did he say?

W of L: Well, he had obviously read it carefully, and began with all the usual nice things. He's been a teacher for decades, he knows what to say, but then . . .

Voice: Then what?

W of L: Well, some of it seemed a bit harsh, but you know, it's exactly what I need to hear right now. Because the things he's objecting to, the metafiction, the feminism, are things I'm going to need to be able to defend —

Voice: Why should you have to defend them?

W of L: Hell, you've read it. You know exactly why.

Scene Four: 3:17 PM Cafeteria. Woman waits, file folder before her. Man sits down, hands woman a book.

M of L: Thanks for the piece on Updike.

W of L: Wasn't it hilarious?

M of L: Yes. Yes, it was.[6]

Scene Five: Same day. 3:37 PM. Man and woman deep in conversation in cafeteria. Two tables away is a younger woman, a former student of the Woman of Letters, sitting alone, reading. Zoom in to Woman of Letters clearly offering something. Man of Letters waves her away, refuses the offer

---

[6] David Foster Wallace's savaging of John Updike's novel is collected in his book of essays titled *Consider the Lobster*. In the essay, Wallace refers to Updike as a GMN — great male narcissist — and finds that the central flaw of Updike's latest novel is its "bizarre adolescent belief that getting to have sex with whomever one wants whenever one wants to is a cure for human despair" (59). Only after Woman of Letters loaned Man of Letters the piece did she remember that his wife is often referred to by gossips as "Poor Eileen."

of food or drink. She has a pile of notes spread out before her. Man sits across, arms folded.

W of L: Well, no writer can expect to please every reader, and obviously I didn't please you. But that's okay.

M of L: "That's okay?" "You can't please everybody?"

W of L: Yeah. (looks at him)

M of L: You have failed. I don't buy it. It's Russian dolls, nothing in the last one. Why would anyone want to read this?

W of L: Whoa. Come on now, that's a bit harsh.[7]

M of L: What I'm saying is that even if it is just a fantasy, it's *off*. I have spent a lot of time in England, and I can tell you that your portrayal of Leland is just *off*. And you risk boring or losing your reader if your portrait isn't believable, isn't right.[8]

W of L: But she invented him, she's never been to England, all she knows is what she's read and imagined, so —

M of L: Yes, I know, but it's still *off*. And another thing is, so this is just a fantasy, so she's aroused, she's horny . . . so what? On the whole, I'm not sure that metafiction is even relevant here. What if you just got rid of Jay and Leland and focussed on Janet, on her story, and her struggles? That's what really works in this manuscript.

---

[7] Because in the twenty minutes they have spent together, he has gone from "a bit off" to "off" to "not believable" to "doing it badly" to "failure." That's a long slope and she suspects he's gone down it because she has not admitted she was wrong. She has not apologized. She has not cried.

[8] "For Heath Stanford [linguistics professor], a defining feature of 'substantive works of fiction' is unpredictability. She arrived at this definition after discovering that most of the hundreds of serious readers she interviewed have had to deal, one way or another, with personal unpredictability . . . people whose lives haven't followed the course they were expected to: . . . [such as] women whose lives have turned out to be radically different from their mothers'. This last group is particularly large." From "Why Bother?" by Jonathan Franzen, collected in *How to be Alone*.

W of L: But the metafiction *is* the point. I'm getting the feeling that you just plain don't like the form I've chosen or the idea behind it. To me, metafiction is one of the most interesting ways available to interrogate what creativity and literary authority actually mean!

M of L: (thinks) Well, I guess there's *Tristram Shandy.*

W of L: Come on, can't you name a metafictional text you enjoyed that was written in the last century?

M of L: (thinks) Oh I don't know, John Fowles, I guess.

W of L: The movie version was masterful.

M of L: I didn't like the movie, but I believe I quite liked the book.[9]

W of L: What about a metafictional work by a woman?

M of L: (thinks. A long time.) Nothing comes to mind.

W of L: Munro's story "Material"! Or what about *Our Lady of the Lost and Found* by Diane Schoemperlen?

M of L: Canadian. I haven't read them.

W of L: Schoemperlen's book is wonderful, it's infuriating. She keeps butting up against the reader's hunger for narrative, deflecting it, teasing, saying *yeah yeah I know you want to hear what happens next, but here, listen to this first, isn't this amazing?*

M of L: I'm not at all sure that infuriating the reader is what you want to be doing. And anyway, I've always found Munro pretty nasty. To both men and women, really. But particularly to men.

---

[9] "The novelist is still a god, since he creates (and not even the most aleatory avant-garde novel has managed to extirpate its author completely); what has changed is that we are no longer the gods of the Victorian image, omniscient and decreeing; but in the new theological image, with freedom our first principle, not authority." John Fowles, *The French Lieutenant's Woman*, ch. 13, quoted in *On Histories and Stories* by A.S. Byatt.

W of L: Nasty? (Looks away. A longer pause. Turns back, deep breath.) What about Margaret Laurence, then? Her depictions of desire and sexuality in *The Diviners*?

M of L: Laurence gets it wrong. There's something off, the men are shadowy. Really, I think a lot of women writers are quite sexist in their depiction of relationships between men and women. They don't get men right. They don't get sexuality right.

W of L: I, um. Wow. (deep breath, long pause.) You said "a lot of women writers." Can you name a female writer who does get it right then? Sexuality, relationships?

M of L: I'm trying to think.[10]

W of L: What about George Eliot? What about the Brontes? I mean, here you are on at me for inventing this supposedly perfect romance, but isn't that exactly what women novelists do? What Charlotte and Emily did? They had little or no experience, beyond their father and brother, and look what they created!

M of L: I think Emily was a much more hard-minded woman than Charlotte. Much more hard minded[11] than anybody realized.

W of L: Look, one of the very few places you got it right was when you said that okay, maybe I needed the romantic fantasy as a cover, as permission, as a place to hide so I could write this book, so I could say what I said. But I still think that without that layered structure, of fantasy within fantasy, I don't know. It's the very bones of the book.

---

[10] "Those in whom virtues not acquired by their merit, and which they feel unequal to it, inspire humility, are the few and the best few." John Stuart Mill, "The Subjection of Women."

[11] The term "hard-minded" cannot be found in any dictionary.

M of L: I'm telling you it doesn't work. Using metafiction for what is basically just a generic romance.

W of L: (visibly frustrated now, scans her notes, stabs a finger on a typed line) Now here's something I must take exception to. How can you possibly say that the agonizing about the rape fantasy is just an accident of the author's feminism rather than anything significant to do with character? That Jay's just a mouthpiece for some feminist agenda? It's where she lives, it's what she *is*! It's not just . . . for effect, or something. Not some device. I mean, really, was Lily Briscoe just some mouthpiece for Woolf's feminist agenda? Gimme a break.

M of L: (shrugs, then smiles slyly) Now I know that one thing you did want to talk about was the eroticism —

W of L: (pulls back her chair, withdrawing) No, not really. It's not that big an issue with me anymore, now that I've completed this draft. I mean, there I was thinking that this was so racy and then my twenty-one-year-old son apologized, at Halloween, for borrowing an extension cord from my house, because he'd used up all the money for his bondage costume on a ball gag. So I'm thinking, hell, this is nothing.[12]

Scene Six: entrance to the cafeteria. Man and woman saying goodbye.

W of L: Well, thanks for this.

---

[12] "You are right that with me everything ends in great erotic scenes. I have the feeling that a scene of physical love generates an extremely sharp light which suddenly reveals the essence of characters and sums up their life situation . . . And precisely because it is the deepest region of life the question posed to sexuality is the deepest question. This is why my book of variations can end with no variations but this." Milan Kundera, interviewed by Philip Roth, in the Afterword to the Penguin edition of *The Book of Laughter and Forgetting*.

M of L: (smirking, surprised) You're more than welcome.

An awkward moment, then she reaches up and gives him a clumsy hug. He seems embarrassed.[13]

Scene Seven: Several days later. Women's locker room, college gym. Middle-aged woman approaches Woman of Letters.

MAW: You look tired. How's the work going?

W of L: Well. Not so good. I feel kind of stuck these days. I've actually decided to set the manuscript aside for now. Maybe start something else.[14]

MAW: C'mon. I'm just heading over to the cafeteria for a bowl of soup.

Pan back as the women cross the courtyard, conversation inaudible. Enter the cafeteria.

Cut to Man of Letters at a table at the corner of the café with two other Men of Letters. The two women seat themselves as far away as possible. The occasional loud bursts of laughter from the men's table are audible.

---

[13] Adrienne Rich argues that one of the ways that women sabotage themselves is through "addiction to male approval; as long as you can find a man to vouch for you, sexually or intellectually, you must be somehow all right, your existence vindicated, whatever the price you pay." From her eulogy for Anne Sexton, 1974.

[14] "A second chance — that's the delusion. There never was to be but one. We work in the dark — we do what we can — we give what we have. Our doubt is our passion and our passion is our task. The rest is the madness of art." Henry James, "The Middle Years," quoted in David Lodge's *Author, Author*. Lodge follows this quote with these lines: "He [Henry James] was not quite sure himself exactly what the last two sentences meant; like the speeches of Hamlet or Lear they contained more than any prosaic paraphrase could express. If he were to die tomorrow, he would be happy to have them inscribed on his tombstone."

Scene Eight: Auditorium, five minutes before a literary reading at the college.

Man of Letters stands awkwardly at the entrance, looking overdressed in a sports jacket and tie. (He is the featured reader this evening.) Woman of Letters arrives late and is searching for a place to sit. As she moves up the aisle, Man of Letters catches her eye. Sheepish. Pleading, even. So, as she moves up the aisle to take her seat, she touches his elbow.[15] He is stiff with nervous tension.

W of L: Break a leg, guy.

M of L: (smiles) Thanks.[16]

He approaches the podium and the crowd welcomes him with applause. In the reading, from the first pages of his novel in progress, an expositional passage describes the narrator's precocious lust for the mother of a childhood friend. In the Q&A, nobody asks, "So he's aroused, so what?"

Final Scene: A blank wall, top of chair visible.

W of L: (offscreen) Okay. Is it on? Okay, listen . . . (appears onscreen, sits, faces camera) I lied. Okay? I lied. I did want to

---

[15] "and into this delicious fecundity, this fountain and spray of life, the fatal sterility of the male plunged itself, like a beak of brass, barren and bare. He wanted sympathy." *To the Lighthouse* .

[16] "Here he was, close upon her again, greedy, distraught. Well, thought Lily in despair, letting her right hand fall at her side, it would be simpler then to have it over. Surely she could imitate from recollection the glow, the rhapsody, the self-surrender she had seen on so many women's faces (on Mrs. Ramsay's for instance) when on some occasion like this they blazed up — she could remember the look on Mrs. Ramsay's face — into a rapture of sympathy, of delight in the reward they had, which, though the reason of it escaped her, evidently conferred on them the most supreme bliss of which human nature was capable. Here he was, stopped by her side. She would give him what she could." *To the Lighthouse.*

seduce him. But not sexually. I wanted him to be bowled over, I wanted not his blessing, but my *power*. Over him. I wanted a place at the table. Did you notice all the tables Jay comes to? Just a place at the table. The grownup's table, too. I never seem to be invited to sit with the grownups. It pisses me off. And I don't want to be invited or asked. Or made a place. I have a place. At the table. It's mine, goddammit.[17] (looks intently into camera lens for a very long time.) Okay. That's it, then. (rises, moves off screen.)

Blank wall, chair top. A clicking sound.
Black.

---

[17] "Writing is a form of personal freedom. It frees us from the mass identity we see in the making all around us. In the end, writers will write not to be outlaw heroes of some underculture but mainly to save themselves, to survive as individuals." Don De Lillo, quoted in "Why Bother?"

APPENDIX # 2: EPILOGUE

A letter arrived, about a year after my novel came out. Forwarded by the publisher of the book you, the reader, now hold in your hands.[18] "It's the weirdest thing," the letter begins, "a friend recommended your novel to me, someone who was tired of hearing me complain that women mystify me. And so I opened the book and a few pages in I read of this young girl being rescued from a party on a Gulf Island. The incident you described resonated deeply with me, reminded me of a night and a morning I spent many years ago when I was living near the ferry landing on Quadra. Can you guess where this is headed? The author photo on the cover of your book, well. There's no mistake. Don't know what to say next. Except maybe that it's kind of cool to know that I have been remembered in this way."

And my first thought was *No! he's probably bald and holier/ hippier than thou and I don't know, an accountant or something. No, I want to go back to the airport with the Englishman, I want to say, "Don't get on that plane, don't go, let's go back to Richdale, just one more day, no two —"*

Several months and many emails later, I meet the honest man who whisked me away from the party at the A-frame all those years ago. At Comox airport he is eager but wary, a burly guy with thinning reddish-blond hair. We have coffee,

[18] Or listen to as an audio book or gaze at on a screen.

and after an hour or two of conversation, I say, "I'd like to see your place. Is it far away?"

We get in his pickup and twenty minutes later drive up to a two-and-a-half storey cedar house in a clearing surrounded by old growth forest. He stops the truck and a dog barks at the top of the stairs. Yes. The double stairs from my dream. All my bright chatter falls away.

"Ah," is all I can manage. Drop my head, massage my temple.

He gets out, walks around to the passenger side and gently swings open the door. When I look up again, I think I glimpse a black cat in a window of the house, rubbing itself seductively against a windowpane. The man just allows me to gape, says gently, "The ground floor's my studio. The living area's upstairs."

But I don't move, not for a long time. He waits patiently. He is a patient man.

Introducing author JM in A LUCID DREAM See how JM is inspired to craft her stunning novel called A HAPPY PRISONER in which JANET MAIR, author of a previous story collection, is now in the throes of creating her debut novel FINAL DRAFT about JAY MCNAIR, author of Richdale and Definition. How do these three stories intertwine? Only you, reader, can find out. Introducing author JM in A LUCID DREAM See how JM is to craft her stunning novel called A HAPPY PRISONER in which JANET MAIR author of a previous story collection, is now in throes of creating her debut novel FINAL DRAFT about JAY MCNAIR author of Richdale and Definition. How do these three stories intertwine? Only you reader, can find Introducing author JM A LUCID DREAM See how

CAST

JM
her SON (12)
her lover, THE MAN WHOSE TEETH DON'T
MATCH
her past lovers, TWO HONEST MEN
her imagined lover, *HIM*

JANET MAIR
her children, DARCE, MATT, & ERIC
her former father-in-law, MOE
her lover, RAY (aka MISTER SUNSHINE)
her imagined lover, *THE ENGLISHMAN*
(a famous author)

JAY MCNAIR
her sons, BEN (17) & DANNY (12)
her mother, MARA
her lover, LELAND MACKENZIE
her other lover, GRAY

JoAnn McCaig is a very bookish person, and is the author of a novel, *The Textbook of the Rose,* and of a critical study, *Reading In: Alice Munro's Archives.* She taught university English for many years and now is the co-owner of an independent bookstore in Calgary.